THE
HOPE STORE

a novel

Dwight Okita

The First Edition was published in May 2017 through Kindle Direct Publishing. The Second Edition was published through CreateSpace in August 2017 and includes vintage drawings and character avatars in the book's interior.
The font is Garamond 14.

I dedicate this book to those
who love to read novels and live alternate lives.
Without you, I am shouting into the void.

And to those amazing people
who make my life fun and worth living.
I see you at my slumber parties
and I see you in my dreams.

SYNOPSIS

Two Asian American men, Luke and Kazu, discover a bold new procedure to import hope into the hopeless. They vow to open the world's first Hope Store. Their slogan: "We don't just instill hope. We *install* it." The media descend. Customer Jada Upshaw arrives at the store with a hidden agenda, but what happens next no one could have predicted. Meanwhile an activist group called *The Natural Hopers* emerges warning that hope installations are a risky, Frankenstein-like procedure and vow to shut down the store.

Luke comes to care about Jada, and marvels at her Super-Responder status. But in dreams begin responsibilities, and often unimaginable nightmares soon follow. If science can't save Jada, can she save herself -- or will she wind up as collateral damage?

WORKS BY DWIGHT OKITA

NOVELS
THE PROSPECT OF MY ARRIVAL
Finalist in the Amazon Breakthrough Novel Awards

THE HOPE STORE
The book you're holding in your hands

EVERY TIME WE SAY GOODBYE
Novel-in-progress about love, reincarnation & gun control

POETRY
CROSSING WITH THE LIGHT
Poetry book, Tia Chucha Press

Various poems have been reprinted in the following: *Norton Introduction to Poetry*, ACM (Another Chicago Magazine), Hyphen Magazine, Breaking Silence (Greenfield Review Press), *Premonitions* (Kaya Production), Nit & Wit, *Unsettling America* (Penguin), *Celebrate America in Poetry and Art* (Smithsonian/Hyperion), and textbooks by Holt Rinehart Winston, McGraw-Hill, Pearson, Bedford/St. Martin's, and Macmillan among others.

PLAYS
RICHARD SPECK
Commissioned & produced by American Blues Theatre

THE RAINY SEASON
Produced by Zebra Crossing Theatre/North Avenue Productions, published in Asian American Drama, *Applause Books*

THE SPIRIT GUIDE
Selected & presented at the HBO New Writers Project

CONTENTS

PERIL

1. I Come Unarmed
2. Boomerang
3. Garden Variety
4. A Guided Tour
5. What Matters
6. Superstitious
7. An Imaginary Life
8 The Epidemic
9. Party Crasher
10. Tsunami
11. A Parallel World
12. Shame On You
13. Important Meetings
14. Small Humans

RESURRECTION

15. Our Public Awaits Us
16. Evil Spirits
17. Audition
18. The Magnetic Moment
19. Check-In
20. Weeks of Wonder
21. Complex

22. At The Movies
23. A Dimming
24. Hopers in Transition
25. You Are Here
26. Doghouse
27. Famous
28. Fancy People
29. A Tiny Paper World

QUANDARY

30. Wide Awake
31. Pre-Heated
32. When You Believed
33. Lovers and Lawyers
34. A Good Man
35. Encore
36. Portal
37. A Tough Room
38. Loose Cannons
39. A Parallel Girl
40. Lucky People
41. A Private Person
42. Close Your Eyes
43. Still Here
44. Chopper

PERIL

"They say these evenings open up like parachutes
and each night someone is saved: by string,
white silk filling with air, snagging on the sky."

-- from the poem "Parachute"

"Please excuse my daughter from school. She does not feel well. She may never feel well again."

JADA

1. I COME UNARMED

My name is Jada Upshaw.

I started out as a girl without dreams and grew up to be a woman without a future.

Mind you, it's not a story I'm especially proud to tell, but if I'm at a party and someone asks me what my story is, that's what I tell them. It's a conversation stopper all right, but whatcha gonna do?

In my teenage years, I was diagnosed with a rare condition called *desina sperara* which means I was "born without the breath of hope." (If you say desina sperara quickly, you can see where the word *desperate* comes from.) My condition has something to do with a breakdown in the brain's reward system. My shrink says I have to work harder to process and

1

pursue rewarding experiences, but basically, it means my pleasure center is totally shot and the act of hoping is just not in my bag of tricks.

Despite my impairment, I managed to get a degree in graphic design (I liked the idea of making the world look more beautiful than it really is) and for a decade I held a job at a bank doing mind-numbing print ads about IRAs and ATMs. I'd still be there if it wasn't for my catastrophic hope breakdown which led experts to say, "Put this woman on disability! Pronto!"

For those of you still listening, my name is pronounced JAY-duh -- as in jaded, as in been there /done that/won't be doing it again anytime soon. Today is the kind of dreary fall morning that Chicago can be so famous for -- dark and foreboding with 78% chance of rain. I'm sitting near the windows at Rendezvous Cafe nursing my Plain Jane latte, spending money I don't have. Though I'm surrounded by an army of laptops, I come unarmed and in peace, unless you count the two precious children, Angie and Willis, by my side as weapons as I sometimes do. They're my sister's kids and she conned me into taking them out in public by paying me three times my normal babysitting fee. I think she got the better end of the deal.

Out of the corner of my eye, I see the kids have decided to sit down at a table with a complete stranger. Lovely. I feel the need to save the man. I walk over to his table. "Uh, guys, seriously. You can't just plop yourselves down at this nice man's table without asking."

The man seems more amused than annoyed. "I don't mind. Cute kids," he says and proceeds to type on his Mac.

"Yeah, they're not mine," I say and smile. I yank them gently back to my table and order mocha iced lattes to keep them occupied.

From time to time the man steals a glance at me. I guess I look all right for a forty-something woman. I have long straightened hair (thanks to a Spoil Me Salon gift certificate) and pleasant enough features. Picture Mary Tyler Moore if she were African-American and you're getting warm, though I'm not likely to throw my hat up into the air no matter how, uh, you know, uh, what's the word, *exuberant* I may feel. (If you're too young to remember Mary Tyler Moore, google her. She's an important part of our collective TV history.) I don't think I've ever been accused of being exuberant, but I can flash a smile on the outside even when I'm feeling nothing on the inside. Still, at a party, I'd be easy to overlook. You might look at me and say, "Now here's a woman with no story to tell," but you'd be wrong. My deep brown eyes see everything. There's no hiding from eyes like these.

My goal today is to enjoy my coffee on this cool fall day, write two pages in my journal, and keep the kids from trashing the place. I open my spiral notebook and pull out a pen. I stare at the blank white page but nothing comes. Suddenly, I feel I'm being watched.

"You know what your problem is, Aunt Jada?" says Angie. "You don't have any self steam. My teacher is teaching us to build up our self steam." Willis nods supportively.

I smile at them. "Self steam, huh? Maybe I need to go back to school and get some of that myself." I know she meant to say self-esteem but why correct her? Every person needs a healthy dose of self steam to get their engine running.

Eventually the kids start to slow down. Willis and Angie are quietly drawing pictures on their paper placemats and that's just fine with me. My eyes wander over to a huge poster that fascinates me. It is of the Sutro Baths in San Francisco, a huge steel and glass structure from the turn of the century that was considered quite ground-breaking for its day. Large steel and glass structures, especially of this size, had not been built before. They called the structure a naturarium and the water source was actually the Pacific Ocean. Somehow the indoor water pool was connected to the ocean so folks were swimming in real saltwater.

I study the bathers, men and women, in their modest bathing suits. I wonder if I would have been happier in that era. At the Sutro Baths, if a person no longer wanted to swim, no longer wanted to be a part of this world -- all they had to do was stop paddling, stop fighting, and just let the water take them. They would sink like a stone to the bottom and never be heard from again. Their bodies would pass through a membrane and float out to sea.

Last night when I was getting ready for bed I saw a story on CNN that caught my attention. There's a scientist -- an Asian guy, some mad scientist type with a pocket protector -- working on a new technique for increasing the amount of hope in hopeless people. To him, I say *Good luck with that, sir. But don't expect me to hold my breath for a miracle.* It takes a while for a new procedure to get the FDA seal of approval.

By then, I'll be dead. I plan to have checked out of the Hotel of Life. If things go according to plan, I should be history before the start of the new year...just three months away. One-third the time it takes to make a baby. Three small pages torn from a wall calendar, and then it's adios.

"Those who start life hopeless rarely acquire it later on. Those who are hopeful in their early years can sometimes lose hope. Can hopefulness be acquired? Can it be conjured or created? Some scientists think so."

-- AlternaScience Magazine

LUKE

2. BOOMERANG

My name is Luke Nagano.

I came into this world as a boy with a big heart but no idea where to put it.

In kindergarten during nap time we spread our blankets on the cold linoleum floor. Donna, a blond girl with short bangs, kept staring at me as we napped. Finally, she smiled at me and said, "Aren't you gonna talk? You got to talk sometime." I pretended to be sleeping, but I heard her loud and clear. In order for me to speak, however, I had to have the corresponding hope that I had something interesting to say.

I didn't know it then but I was in for a life of mild hope impairment that would limit me in ways I couldn't predict. I did, in fact, start talking. I dove deep down into myself and metamorphosed into a respectable ambivert… almost through sheer brute force. It took years for me to learn how to throw my voice out into the world and wait for it to come boomeranging back to me.

But today is a new day…a sparkling, clear October morning. I can see sunlight peeking in through the powder-blue Levelor blinds. It might rain but so what? I'm a *pluviophile,* a rain worshipper. Already in my mid-thirties, most people peg me as twenty-something. (Thanks for the genes, Mom and Pop!) Kazu just hit forty but age is truly just a number when you believe in reincarnation. He's a card-carrying Buddhist. I fall more into the undeclared spirituality zone.

I find myself waking up a few hours earlier than I usually do. Kazu is still asleep under the silver pinstriped bedspread. *I am up to something.* On the living room wall, I begin to hang a banner made from butcher block paper which reads:

THE HOPE STORE.
We don't just instill hope. We *install* it.

Once I heard a politician jabbering on the six o'clock news and he said: "We have to install hope in young people!" He meant to say "instill," but it was funnier the way he said it. Creepier too. And that was the seed of my slogan. I love it. I reach up and touch the paper, touching it as if it were alive. A much nicer version of this banner will be hung in the store when we open our doors next week, but this is just for fun. This is just to surprise Kazu who appears to be deep in the REM stage. Kazu Mori is my partner, in more ways than I can name. Soulmate would be one of his monikers.

In just a week, we will open the first store in the world to sell hope over the counter.

This is going to be big.

It gives whole new possibilities to those who are born with hope impairment and those whose hope supplies have eroded over time due to disappointment, disillusion, and brain chemistry disorders. Chartreuse Johnson is the main investor in The Hope Store and a smart cookie. She's also a tough cookie. She's made it clear that the store has got to be an overnight sensation if we want to continue receiving her investor checks. She's giving us three months: October, November, and December. So we have to make our mark in the world and leave a big footprint -- or we're toast, we go belly-up, and The Hope Store reverts to the Starbucks it once was.

What do you want out of a store? An iced latte or an extra dose of hope? I know. Decisions, decisions.

★

The day I first walked into LiveWell Laboratories, I went looking for answers. I had heard there was a new clinical trial to increase hope in the hope-challenged. I was enthralled. And what did I have to lose but my dignity? My job as a textbook editor paid my rent and covered my indulgent movie-going habit, but I didn't feel it was my calling. So it was a pleasure to meet Kazu Mori, scientist extraordinaire. Young by any measure, he had more prizes and awards for his scientific endeavors than could fit on the long shelf in his office. He was sure of himself and his purpose. And he was super cute. A tall Asian man, his long shiny black hair and clean-shaven face were in stark contrast to my buzzed head and the soul patch on my chin.

If he came across as a rock star scientist on the verge of greatness...I came across more as an artist-in-residence on the verge of being discovered. At 5'6" I was compact, proving once again that good things come in small packages. Sometimes guys described me as a teddy bear, but the men I dated never stayed more than a year...no matter how nice I was to them.

Though I was Japanese American (still am, by the way), it was hard to find a Japanese bone in my body -- aside from my love of sushi and Zen rock gardens and films by Nagisa Ôshima. My face was unmistakably Japanese -- the Epicanthic folds of my eyes, the humble nose -- but when I opened my mouth, only American ideas poured out. Kazu was born and bred in Tsukuba, Japan; I hailed from Chicago, Illinois. I read online somewhere that if I ever took a trip to Japan, I'd be shunned as a foreigner. I was like a baby bird that had fallen from its nest -- forever tainted by American ideas.

The rock star scientist guided me past the many rooms of LiveWell with glass windows longer than a stretch limousine. Signs on the doors read: "Bio-Experiment in Progress." In one room a woman was running on a treadmill. There were three signs on the walls around her which announced: NEED, WANT, HOPE. As she ran, the signs on the walls began to move, to re-arrange themselves. "I don't know what any of this means, but I'm dying to find out," I said. "I can be patient and wait for the official start of the clinical trials."

"You have great self-control," said Kazu with a grin. "I like that. Let me tease you further by showing you my favorite room of all -- the room where it happens."

We watched through the long glass window as a man sat as if upon a throne, his whole body encircled by a halo of white light. Confetti began to trickle down on him, but it wasn't the kind you see in parades. This confetti was shiny and fell in dream-like slow motion. What struck me was the expression on the man's face. He looked ecstatic, like he had just learned something that would change his life forever. If that's what it looked like to have hope installed -- I wanted to know that feeling too. I wanted to feel it right away.

JADA

3. GARDEN VARIETY

Some people might think I'm morbid, looking at a beautiful poster of the Sutro Baths in a coffee-house and thinking of how people might end their lives. I prefer to think of myself as unfiltered. Porous.

I suspect a whole lot of people with hope deficits go undiagnosed, and still others are misdiagnosed as having garden variety depression, and god knows you don't have to have desina sperara (DS) to be hope-impaired. You can be born hopeless, and you can become hopeless. Some people believe you can catch hopelessness just by sitting next to a stranger on a train. Not true. I myself have learned I am immune to the charms of antidepressants, talk therapy, hypnosis and homeopathic remedies, so I've pretty much been in free fall for my adult life. I often fantasize about the most painless way to kill myself. In my life, I've tried to kill myself twice. Here's hoping the third time's the charm.

I really would like to be happy and hopeful like other earthlings but I don't see it happening in this lifetime. So I'm doing this babysitting gig with my sister Sheila's two offspring, Willis and Angie. On this particular Saturday, their parents have snuck out to see a movie. The little rascals are opening countless packets of Splenda and sprinkling them into their iced lattes. I figure it's never too early to introduce caffeine to children. I don't hate kids. I just think all children are loud and unpredictable and too high-maintenance.

Maybe I'm just cranky. I haven't had a good night's sleep in decades and that's bound to take a toll. We could trade bodies for a week, but trust me, you don't want to know. When I worked at the bank, there were days I didn't have anything to do. I'd sit at my desk and I could feel my bones morphing, turning to stone. And that was on a good day. Thank god Otis Franklin took a shine to me, though I have no idea why.

Angie, for reasons that are not apparent to me, has decided to punch her older brother in his privates. "Angie, don't hit your brother in his special place! If you do that -- he won't be able to have babies," I say. Then add, "Not that it matters much to me, but your parents probably have an opinion about that."

"About what?" Willis asks.

"About everything. That's what parents do. They have opinions. Now sit down and drink your iced lattes before they melt. Aunt Jada wants to write in her journal. Is that too much to ask?" Now, where was I? Oh yeah, so I have a man in my life who loves me exactly as I am. And many of my single, middle-aged girlfriends are envious. But here's the killing part. I can't love him back! Not the way he deserves to be loved. I'm numb. Loving someone back just isn't in my repertoire. I'm The Girl Who Wasn't There. Sometimes, because I can put on a good face, people think I'm happy. Now that's what I call LOL funny. If you were to send a probe into the very inside of me, you'd see: The mall is open, but nobody's shopping.

When our time at Rendezvous Cafe finally comes to an end, I look down at my spiral notebook and all I see are a few stray sentences scribbled on the page. Not even close to the two pages I had hoped to fill.

Dear Angie and Willis,

I am a walking cautionary tale. Don't grow up to be me, whatever you do. Be happy and hopeful. That's more fun. By the time you read this, I will be a distant memory.

Aunt Jada

I close my notebook and decide to stop at the ladies room before we leave. The kids say they don't have to visit the bathroom so I ask that nice man with the Mac if he'd mind terribly keeping an eye on the darlings for a hot second.

"No problem," he says. He seems kind, probably a father himself. And a Mac user to boot.

In the washroom, I notice the nice, plum-scented incense that wafts through the room. I wonder who makes it. Then I start to wonder: Was it dumb of me to leave the kids in the hands of a perfect stranger? He said they were 'cute kids.' I rush back to the heart of the coffeehouse.

All I see is my spiral notebook on the table where I left it.

The kids and the man are nowhere to be seen.

LUKE

4. A GUIDED TOUR

I was flattered that day Kazu took me on a guided tour of the legendary LiveWell Laboratories. Did he treat all subjects for clinical trials like this? He showed me around the premises as if I was a VIP, pointing out secret rooms and scientific equipment, introducing me to his colleagues along the way. I remember the walls of one hallway flickered with illuminated images of brain hemispheres, functional MRI (fMRI) images showing a colorful river tracing the exuberance of brain activity -- the release of neurotransmitters, temperature, blood flow, sparks of electricity. But the images were not still; the colors moved in slow motion as if their energy could not be contained.

One brain portrait showed the brain illuminated like a blue lightbulb with splatters of yellow scattered throughout. Underneath was the subheading:
"This is the brain liking something."

Another portrait showed the brain as a pitch-black sky with red and white meteorites descending earthward:

"This is the brain expressing fear."

The image shows the brain with hula hoops of blinding white light at its center. The hoops glimmer against a background of purple and green:

"This is the brain hoping for something."

Every picture told a story with bursts of color here and there. It was as if the pictures were saying: "If you really want to understand the human story -- follow the light show."

Kazu walked me past the many conference rooms. Signs on the doors read: CLINICAL TRIAL IN PROGRESS. But through the glass, I could still make out silhouettes moving, a facilitator pointing to a flip chart. It was all very exciting to me somehow for soon I would be on the other side of the door. I would be a participant in a clinical study. I remember one sign by the coffee machine read: "Be Open To Anything... But Question Everything."

In another room, a woman was in a small theater, her eyes fixed on a movie screen. On the screen was the same woman: It is her wedding day. Someone is making a toast. Then the image stutters, pixilates, goes dark. Another image appears on-screen. The woman is wearing a bathing suit adorned with images of red tulips. She immerses herself in a bathtub filled with steaming water. She slides her body down lower and lets the water take her. The image stutters, pixilates, goes dark.

I didn't know it at the time but I was the only volunteer whom Kazu favored with such a personal tour. Later after the study was over, he told me he gave me a tour partly because I had arrived an hour early, yes, but also because he wanted to. "I was extremely drawn to you for some reason," he confessed.

I wondered what it was about me he was drawn to, but I didn't want to ask. I wanted to groove on the ambiguity. Was it my smile, my curiosity? Did he find me fetching, to his fancy, a studmuffin? Or was it just my overall Lukeness that he found irresistible? One day I would ask him these questions.

But today is not that day, I thought to myself.

JADA

5. WHAT MATTERS

My eyes scan the tables at the Rendezvous Cafe.

I don't see Angie and Willis anywhere.

I try not to panic. I walk up to the counter to talk to the waitress with the hot pink hair. "Excuse me, did you happen to see the two small children that were with me?" But now I see the waitress is on the phone, taking a delivery order. She hasn't heard a word I've said. The coffee house is fuller than I remember. People in the cafe are laughing like hyenas, are jabbering.

Just then the nice man steps out from behind a shelving unit. It's where they display bags of freshly ground coffee of various flavors. "There you are," the man says to me, and I breathe a sigh of relief.

Then I see the kids appear, one by one, each holding a bag of coffee in their hands. "Aunt Jada, can we bring some coffee home for Mommy and Daddy?" asks Willis. They raise their bags high over their cute little heads so I can examine them. I don't think I've ever been so glad to see them in my life.

"Just pick one bag, kids," I say. I thank the man for watching the kids. I am overly gushy in my gratitude because in my mind I am also thanking him for not being a pedophile or a serial killer. I am thanking him for restoring a bit of my faith in humanity, however small.

Suddenly the stranger's face lights up. "Hey, do you want to trade information? Maybe we could grab coffee sometime."

"Oh, that's okay. I'm kind of a private person," I say.

"I just watched your kids for you."

"They're not mine."

"Yeah, you said that. It's a new millennium, Jada. We're all Facebook babies. Privacy is so yesterday." He smiles strangely. I don't like that he knows my name.

"Thanks again for your help," I say. "I really appreciate it."

The man puts a card in my hand and smiles. I hesitate. "Well, don't be rude. At least take my card. Blair Matters. At your service."

Not wanting to be rude, I take the card.

He winks at me. I put his card in my pocket without looking at it

Maybe I'm being paranoid. He's probably just being friendly.

I round up Angie and Willis. We spill out onto Clark Street, leaving the café and the over-friendly man behind. When I get on the bus with the kids, I read the guy's business card. He is a freelance writer. Not once in my life have I ever had the need of a freelance writer.

I don't think Mr. Matters will matter much to me.

After I drop off the kids at my sister Sheila's, I head for the animal shelter where I volunteer a couple times a week. I have to clean the cages of the dogs and cats; then I feed them. I know I'm not supposed to play favorites, but I'm partial to the cats. They're kind of weird and in their own world...like me. So I think we're, what do you call it when things are connected but they're not really, they're, uh, what's the word...I forget. Anyway, dogs are sweet but just too damn loving for my taste. I set out the Yummy Chow for the critters when my cell rings. It's Sheila. I put her on speaker phone so I can continue with my chores.

"Jada, thanks again for the hazelnut coffee," she says. "That was so thoughtful of you."

"No problem." There is a tiny pause. I reach in and pet the tiniest Calico kitten because she's the shyest of the bunch.

"Say, do you think we can we get together sometime?" Sheila asks. "I'd like to catch up with you." My sister is not the let's-get-coffee-and-gab kind of gal so I'm suspicious.

"Sure. Is there something you want to –"

"Not really," Sheila says. "Well, actually there is. But I'd rather talk to you in person."

"Now you're making me nervous. What is this about?" I say. I stop fussing with the animals. There is a longish pause you could drive a truck through.

Finally Sheila speaks. "Angie showed me the letter you wrote."

"The letter? What letter?" I go to my locker and pull out my bag, dig out my spiral notebook. I flip to the page where I scribbled those notes at the coffeehouse.

The page has been torn out.

"It's the one where you tell them you're a cautionary tale. And that by the time they read the note, you'll be a distant memory. Does that ring a bell?"

I am not happy. "Gosh darn it, Sheila, I did not give that to her."

"Right. Well, Angie said when you guys were at the cafe, she was curious what you were scribbling. When you stepped away, she took at peek."

"Did she now?" I say trying to hide my annoyance.

"And by the way, Jada, if the situation ever arises again, please don't let a strange man watch them. Just bring the kids with you into the washroom. I do it all the time."

"He wasn't *that* strange. But okay."

Sheila continues, as she often does. "Angie was excited to find a letter addressed to her. She thought she was saving you a stamp."

"You know, that is not okay with me, Sheila."

"Jada, love, I really want you to be careful about the things you communicate to my kids. You know they're like sponges."

"Okay, two things I have a problem with. One, the notebook is my personal diary and I don't appreciate anyone peeking at it. And two, are you saying it's okay with you that your child stole something that didn't belong to her?"

`"See, that's exactly why I wanted to talk to you in person --"

"There's nothing to discuss, Sheila. Nothing."

I hear her start to speak, try to reason with me: "Jada, don't be like –" But I hang up my cell anyway.

A moment later, my phone is ringing. I can see it's Sheila but I'm not picking up. Besides, I'm at work. When I take my break, I check the message and hear my sister's voice: "I'm sorry that Angie took your paper. I am. And of course, I told her that she shouldn't take things without asking permission. But you know it's bigger than that, don't you? What I really wanted to know about is...well, are you okay, Jada? I mean...you're not having those thoughts again, are you?"

That's the thing about secrets. Once you tell a secret, there's no way of taking it back, of un-telling it. Ever since that night I told her I was thinking of killing myself – she's looked at me differently. Like I'm a bug in a jar and I'm her new science project.

LUKE

6. SUPERSTITIOUS

I choose to let Kazu get his beauty rest. I walk into the bathroom and greet myself in the mirror. I've been told I look and act younger than my thirty-something years and for that I must thank my good family genes. The hair brush I am holding is Kazu's. My hair is always buzzed short; his hair is long like a pirate's. I close the cabinet and there I am again in the mirror. Gripping the brush tenderly, I speak into it: "I'd like to thank my late, great parents who always told me I could grow up to be anything I wanted to be. I'm just sorry they're not here to see this moment. I'd like to thank biotech companies all over the planet for not being smart enough to discover the secret of creating hope before we did. And most of all I'd like to thank Kazu for..."

In Latin, my name Luke means "bringer of light." Kazu always likes to say that people are born with certain destinies, that our karma is imprinted in our genetic code. He's a Buddhist so he also believes that our destinies are changeable, are works in progress. At the store we have our defined roles. I plan to handle the marketing; Kazu will handle the science. Put another way, it's my job to get customers to walk in the front door; it's his job to keep them coming back. Three years of clinical trials have produced a compelling number of hope-enhanced subjects who will be happy to sing the praises of our scientific endeavor and their breath-taking results. These results are quantifiable and we're thrilled to have finally received our FDA approval.

In the mirror, I see tiny red lines on the whites of my eyes. Are they bloodshot? I haven't been getting much sleep lately. I'm too jazzed about the store opening. But I can't have bloodshot eyes for next week's grand opening. I reach for the Red-Out and let the medicine drops splash onto my eyeballs. Better. Now where was I? Oh, yeah. Kazu. I pick up the hair brush again. "And I'd especially like to thank Kazu Mori for...let's see...what did he do anyway? Hmm. He said I shouldn't hope for much in life or I'd just be disappointed." I grab a tissue and dab the excess moisture from my eyes. "Come to think of it -- I don't think I should thank Kazu for --"

Suddenly a projectile sails into the tiny bathroom and hits me square on the head. It is a small pillow. From the other room, he lets out a thunderous, lion-like yawn. As his eyes gradually adjust to the sunlight filling the apartment, he notices the banner. Suddenly he starts ripping everything down. I run toward Kazu to intervene.

"What the hell are you doing?" I shout.

"You can't --" he starts to speak, then goes back to attacking my banner. I try to place myself in front of it. "You should never --" Kazu proceeds to tear the banner into smaller and smaller pieces.

"Either finish your sentences -- or stop fucking with my banner!" I say. Too late. What remains of the banner will find its way into the recycle bin downstairs.

"Don't you know," he begins, "it's bad luck...to post the advertising slogan for a store before the store opens?" He sits down on the edge of the bed. He seems spent.

"Kazu, that is about the dumbest thing I ever heard."

"It's the worst way to jinx a new business. The worst. I could tell you stories. About an elevator company and elevator cars plunging one hundred feet per second. It isn't pretty."

"I know you're superstitious, but this is ridiculous. Even for you."

"Even for me?" he asks.

"I didn't...you know what I mean!" I say. "You're the one that should be doing the explaining." And now a hush falls over the room. We are either pausing to reload, or considering a ceasefire. "Kazu, we open next week. Do you really want to spend this weekend having a knock-down, drag-out fight?"

"You're right."

"I was trying to surprise you," I say shaking my head. "I didn't know it was bad luck. Is this one of your crazy superstitions?" I considered myself a devout agnostic, while Kazu is a card-carrying Buddhist.

"Actually, it's something I picked up from a business class at Seattle U. I took it as an elective for my PhD in biotech."

"Oh," I say out loud, but inside I'm thinking Seattle folk drink way too much coffee for their own good.

"I'm sorry I snapped at you," Kazu says "Come here." He pulls me into a gentle bear hug. "It's nerves. I just want our opening to be a smash. I take after my mother. She gets very hyper when she entertains."

"I'm nervous too," I confess. Then Kazu does the thing. It's the one thing I can't resist, an absolute power that he has over me. He uses his magic thumbs and kneads the tight muscles of my neck in a way that makes me melt. I am Japanese American; I was born in Chicago in the Hyde Park area. Kazu is Japanese Japanese; he was born in Kyoto in a prefecture. When strangers see us together on the street, they sometimes think we're brothers. If they only knew! At moments like this I believe Kazu is drawing on centuries of Japanese healing mojo and I am happy to be the beneficiary of such an inheritance. Everything wrong in the world becomes pretty close to right when the magic thumbs come out.

And for a moment, it's almost peaceful again in our household. If it weren't for the images flickering through my brain of elevator cars plunging through elevator shafts at the speed of light – I could almost drift back to sleep.

We sit at the kitchen table eating a festive Saturday breakfast: waffles with ripe strawberries and vanilla ice cream. Kazu checks his phone messages and I sketch out some marketing ideas for a Halloween promotion. We both agree 25% off is enticing as it drops the regular price from $1,000 to $750. Until we are a known quantity in Chicago with a loyal following, we need to give people good reasons to check out our services.

Kazu and I have been together for three years now. Long enough to feel completely comfortable with each other; not long enough to take each other for granted. Still, with the launch of The Hope Store just days away, all we can do is talk shop. "You said you could tell me stories about unlucky store openings," I say. "I'm all ears."

"I don't want to scare you," he says looking at me with his soulful, black-as-coal eyes.

"Try me."

"Some stories are better left untold," Kazu says. "All I'll say is one incident involved an elevator company, their brand-new slogan, and a very tragic accident. The owner put up the logo of the company in some of his elevators *before* the company actually opened its doors and boom – tragedy. Very bad luck."

"Could've been a coincidence." I spear a strawberry with my fork.

"If it just happened in one elevator, maybe. But the cables snapped in all three elevators bearing the new slogan -- taking the lives of the owner and several board members," he says. "The two elevators without slogans were fine. Needless to say, the company never opened."

"Here's the weird part for me. How do you reconcile your belief in superstition and your belief in science?"

Kazu laughs. "First of all, I don't call it superstition. That's an American concept. Growing up in Japan, I learned that the world can be divided into the Knowable World and the Unknowable World. These worlds are not contradictory; they're complementary. Westerners have a hard time with that. Westerners want answers that are either black or white. Easterners accept that sometimes the answer is both black *and* white."

"I love it when you get all trippy on me." I lean over and kiss Kazu on his lips which taste of vanilla ice cream. Then I lean over and kiss him again.

"Two kisses? My argument must have been very persuasive."

I take our plates and rinse them in the sink. "I'm still not convinced that my banner needed to be destroyed. Besides, does tearing it down stop the bad luck, or is the bad luck already in motion? Like an arrow shooting through time and space?"

"Time will tell," Kazu says without a hint of irony in his voice. "Let's see how the opening goes before we count our chickens."

JADA

7. AN IMAGINARY LIFE

Living without hope for the past forty-some years is kind of like wandering through a dark cave the size of the Grand Canyon with bats flapping overhead and not having a flashlight to your name. It's a mystery to me how I survived this long, though I'm sure that bravery had nothing to do with it. Last year, I almost didn't. Survive, that is. That was the last time I tried to kill myself.

It was one of those sunless, winter days Chicago is so famous for. Even the laser beams of my SAD light box could not reach me. I found myself again falling down the rabbit hole. I started to fall behind on my mortgage payments, the collection department kept harassing me, and that's when I made up my mind: *I know what I have to do.* I remember laying down my wallet and keys on the kitchen table and breathing a heavy sigh. I would leave a note so people wouldn't have to wonder. A colorful flock of origami paper cranes encircled my belongings on the table, as if paying their last respects. They swam upon a body of water as imaginary as my own life. Where did I find the energy to fold all those paper creatures? I had no idea.

Every time those collection goons called and left a message on my machine, I got a sick feeling in the pit of my stomach as if a piece of fruit was rotting inside me. I was born without that talent for hoping, and now they were coming for the roof over my head. A girl can just give up just so much. I would sooner live in a homeless shelter than feel like an intruder camping on the sofa at Sheila's. But a shelter would probably not allow me the luxury of keeping my cat. What would happen to Shadow? I couldn't give her back to a shelter. That's where I got her in the first place.

I stood facing the eggshell-white walls of my living room. I would leave a note to the world, but what would I say? I thought and thought and then it came to me:

NO ONE KILLED ME. I HAD A BAD DAY
WHICH TURNED INTO A BAD LIFE.

I spray-painted my message in midnight blue. That way no one could overlook the note, or let it fall behind the furniture. I stepped up onto a wooden chair and put my head through the noose. Okay, it was a leash really...for my faithful pet of nine years. Not that you could walk a cat on a leash. Shadow perched on the arm of my paisley sofa and watched me with great interest. My cat could not connect the dots of a chair, a noose, and a desperate woman to see that something terrible was about to happen. She just saw her owner playing with a leash...dancing on a wooden chair.

"Goodbye, Shadow," I said. "Don't worry. Otis will look after you when I'm gone." She licked her front paw with utter indifference. She would not participate in her owner's drama. Shadow didn't care that I played solitaire endlessly on my laptop, that most days I was a few tacos short of a complete fiesta platter. All that she cared about was that I fed her when she was hungry, and petted her when she wanted to be petted.

"Don't eat any more birds. It'll just make you sick again," I said. "Love you, Shadow. You were a great cat. Good-bye." Shadow stopped licking her paw and just stared at me.

I thought of all the disappointments, large and small, in my life. It puzzled me how my boyfriend Otis Franklin could love me when I couldn't even love myself. I thought how much I hated my last job -- back in the days when I had a job. How bored I was at the prison of my desk. How I resented having to make coffee for the monthly staff meetings. "Make your own damn coffee, people," I wanted to scream, but I never screamed. Maybe I should have. Maybe I should have spray-painted my feelings on a wall more often. It might have broken the spell.

Enough. One last look at Shadow. I had thought there would be tears, but there were no tears. I was all cried out. And with that, I closed my eyes and stepped off the chair.

And that should've been the end of me.

The leash cut into my neck like it was going to slice right through. I kicked my legs.

But something broke above me and I crashed to the floor like a clumsy angel. A tiny shower of plaster rained down on me. I hurt all over.

I lay there in a tangle of limbs on the coffee-colored rug. For a moment, I just tried to catch my breath. Otis must never know that I came this close, or I'll never hear the end of it. My throat ached. I rubbed it tenderly. I looked in the mirror and saw rope burn marks. I'd have to wear turtlenecks for a week.

I looked up and saw the new hole in the ceiling.

If anyone asked, I'd say it was there when I moved in. Yes, that was the ticket. I spent the rest of the afternoon putting my home back in order. The cat leash went back into the kitchen drawer. I moved the wooden chair back to the table, swept up the bits of plaster. Argh. The blasted graffiti on the wall. That would take several coats of paint to cover which required a trip to Home Depot. The smell of wet paint would linger for days. Otis would get suspicious of any spontaneous home decoration. I just wouldn't invite him over for a week.

So there is a learning curve, even to dying, I thought to myself.

LUKE

8. THE EPIDEMIC

CARELESS WHISPERS
FROM THE HOPE EPIDEMIC

My hope-endowed, well-intentioned fellow earthlings often ask me: "Aren't hopelessness and depression the same thing?" To which I snarkily reply: "Aren't you and your sibling basically the same person?"

Well...not exactly. I mean, sure, there's a familial resemblance, and you come from the same parents -- but I think you'd agree you're hardly the same person. Not identical twins at all, surely not Siamese twins joined at the hip. Fraternal twins maybe.

So let me make this distinction if I may. If depression is the inability "to feel your life" -- hopelessness is the inability "to do your life." The former has to do with one's emotional repertoire, while the latter has to do with one's behavioral repertoire. Hopeless folks don't have that ambition bird flying in and out of their brains like normal folks. We don't lose a lot of sleep pondering what our true purpose on earth is because we don't think we have a chance in hell of fulfilling said purpose. We're accidental slackers in the most tragic sense. We're beautiful new cars in the auto showroom with no gas in our tanks.

It's not that we've all thrown in the towel. Many of us are trying to rise up. It's more like we're wondering what a towel is, and why didn't we get one. You probably haven't a clue what I'm talking about. Poor hopeful you. At least I appreciate what you were born with, even if you take it for granted.

As I've grown from a hopeless boy into a hopeless man, I've watched as America's greatest natural resource has all but vanished. I'm not talking fossil fuels here, but the innocent ability to have hope in the face of common sense. I can see it in the blank stares of millennials, in the suicide rates, in the relentless gun violence on American streets. Every show on TV is about forensics…the science of how we kill each other. If life doesn't make doesn't matter -- why should death?

I remember a Buddhist buddy giving me some friendly advice in a coffeehouse as we sipped our iced chai lattes: "Luke, it's really as simple as this. Chant for the wisdom to know what to do with your life, and for the courage to act on the wisdom." And though the words were powerful, they fell on deaf ears. Mine.

I only blog when I have something to say or when something unusual happens. Which is to say, I am not a daily or even weekly blogger. I'm sporadic at best. Re-reading this blog brings back a memory.

Kazu told me how his obsession with brain confusion began. He met a doctor in Baltimore at a neurology conference. The woman was doing a radical new procedure she had stumbled upon which proved extremely effective in the treatment of morbid obesity. She had a morbidly obese patient who was actually being treated for brain seizures at the time. The surgeon opened up the man's skull and was delicately touching different parts of the brain with a probe to see if she could duplicate the seizures. The wide-awake patient mentioned that he suddenly felt his ever-present appetite subside for the first time in years. He felt strangely full and sated. After the surgery, when the patient was tempted to overeat, he would again feel full and was no longer hungry. Kazu wondered how else the human brain could be fooled.

"Science is about finding solutions to problems," Kazu said during my clinical trials at LiveWell. "There's a growing epidemic of hopelessness right outside our doors." After some years of exploration, he felt he was finally onto something big. It was a way to trick the brain using magnetic fields into creating more dopamine which, in turn, generated more hope in a patient's brain. It, in fact, created a hope reservoir. That's why this clinical study was on a fast track at LiveWell and why he was excited about the project.

JADA

9. PARTY CRASHER

It's Sunday. I decide to go over to Otis' apartment and hang out with him.

Otis opens the door, and we hug. These days I am more of a hugger than a kisser. "New turtleneck?" he asks.

"Oh, this old thing? I had it lying at the bottom of my closet," I say. The last time I wore it was last year when I tried to hang myself and had to camouflage my purple and black and yellow bruisings around my neck. Ah, memories! This is our Sunday ritual: the newspaper, coffee, maybe something sweet or savory. Today it is savory: sunny-side-up eggs and hash browns. We sit on the sofa reading the Sunday paper, drinking our Orange Cappuccino International Coffee.

"Oh my god," I say without looking up from my section of the paper.

"What?"

"That doesn't make any sense. That sounds too good to be true." I hold the newspaper closer to my face, too lazy get my glasses.

"What sounds too good to be true?" Otis asks.

"There's this new store opening up in Andersonville -- are you ready for this? -- that supposedly sells hope over the counter! Is that the biggest crock of nonsense –"

"Wow. Sounds pretty cool to me. Wonder how it works."

"You wonder how it works? Otis, you think this is for real?" After all these years, Otis' trusting nature still surprises me. "You don't think it's some kind of, uh, uh, you know what I mean, uh, a *scam*?"

"They're making scientific breakthroughs all the time, Jada. Miracles happen every day!"

I just stare at Otis in disbelief. "Yeah, like who wouldn't want to slap down a couple bills and pick up an extra dose of hope? In fact, we might as well load up the Mini Cooper with a year's supply of the stuff while we're at it because I'd probably go through it like I go through a case of Diet Dr. Pepper in a day. And besides, it's what they call, uh, uh, what do they call it? -- when both sides win. Anyway, that thing. At least that's what I'd say if I were normal. But I'm not. I'm hopeless."

Now it's Otis' turn to stare at me so he does. Then he goes back to reading the paper. I can be so darned cynical sometimes. Otis and I, in some ways, are a horrible fit. We are so different in our basic views of the world. When we first met, I found Otis' can-do attitude oddly attractive. And Otis found in me a lost girl who needed to be found.

When I read about this Hope Store and other magic bullets for hopelessness, I just get angry. How much money have I spent on cures that cured me only of my money? Why are these Young Frankensteins profiting off the hopeless and clueless? Where are the consumer advocates that are supposed to be protecting us?

I should do something. In my mind, I hatch a plan. I will to go to The Hope Store and buy whatever they're selling. I will be living proof that their miracle cure won't work, and then I'll tell the world. Till then, this will be my little secret.

I continue to read the article. "Says the creators of the store are Luke Nagano and Kazu Mori," I say. "*Kazu Mori*. Oh my god, I think I know that guy!"

Otis is barely listening. "We could always check out a matinee at the Davis if you like..."

What I fail to mention to Otis is how I know Kazu Mori, if indeed it is the same Kazu Mori. The Kazu I know taught a class on parallel worlds several years ago. Back then, I had a bad afro and never said a peep in class. I had a slight crush on the guy. It's unlikely Kazu would even remember me. I will definitely make a visit to The Hope Store.

"There's a private party for the opening of the store Monday night at 7:00, and the store opens to the public on Wednesday," I announce. "Want to go?

"You just said it's a private party. And besides, you hate parties."

"I don't want to go because it's a party. I want to go because I've never been to a Hope Store. Have you?"

"Fine. Go crash the party and tell me all about it."

I turn to face him. "I'd rather go with you, Otis."

He gives me a look. "I'm not going to get thrown in jail just to satisfy your --"

"Maybe we'll even get a reality show out of it. Like those folks that crashed the White House. What were their names? The Martini's. The Zamboni's? I can never remember names."

"The Salahi's," he says.

"The Salahi's! You have such a good memory, Otis. You should get on a game show and win us a lot of money. I'll just call them the Salami's. If I can eat it, I can remember it."

"You're talking about food and here we just ate."

"I need to use your computer. There's something I want to check." I power up Otis' laptop and google Kazu Mori. It is indeed the same man who taught that terrific class for the Learning Annex on parallel universes a decade ago. I am happy he has done so well for himself. But I'm sad for me that I have so little to show for my own decade.

"According to the Small Business Administration, a third of all new businesses shut their doors in the first two years of operation. In our current wretched economy, however, that time frame is closer to six months to a year."

-- On the Money magazine

LUKE

10. TSUNAMI

Tonight is the soft opening for The Hope Store. The media are invited but the public is not.

My hope levels have never been higher. My cup runneth over; my synapses are snapping. The investors decided that Monday is the best night for the press opening; Wednesday is the best day for the opening to the general public. I am at the top of my game tonight. The store looks great. When you walk in, what takes your breath away is the floor-to-ceiling water fountain that forms a gentle parenthesis behind the front desk. It is a simple effect with water flowing in a sheet over clear glass. Kazu and I wanted it to suggest the abundance of hope available to people. In the freshly painted walls, one will note the overall color theme is aqua blue and chocolate brown. And once you are in the heart of the store, there is the beautiful vinyl banner which bears our slogan.

Kazu is stationed at the front desk amidst the gently rushing water to greet our guests. He looks handsome in his purple shirt with a Koi fish swimming across the front. Everyone who is anyone is there. Everyone who hopes to be someone is here too. I favor the latter group, not just because I count myself among them, but because they are the underdogs, and because they are our future customers. The store was created for them: people who had yet to fully arrive in this world. Yet here they are, plain as day, as if Kazu and I had hoped them into existence.

I can't remember the last time I've seen so many people trying to look effortlessly hip in one place. The women with their dangly earrings and hieroglyphic tattoos. The men with their gelled hair that creates the illusion of little tsunami waves throughout the room. But beneath the shiny surfaces beat matching shiny hearts. They are friends, future customers, members of the media. They are here to bear witness to history in the making. For my part, I wear a simple black dress shirt that has these words silk-screened in silver across the back: *Ask me about hope.*

Though there is much levity in the air, there is pressure as well. The store's investors have made it abundantly clear that in three short months, The Hope Store needs to show dramatic signs of profit and viability or it will be history. All the more reason I'll be thrilled if CNN really does show up. CNN would be a major coup.

Our patron saint is Chartreuse Johnson...Chartreuse who is both a color and a deep-pocketed investor. We met her by chance through the man who was designing our websites. By day, Chartreuse deals with stocks and bonds, but she's always fancied herself an entrepreneur. She's a beginning investor and we're a beginning start-up so the truth is, we're both taking a chance on each other. It would've been great to have an investor with a track record, but the investors we approached were leery of us. They loved the concept but thought more research was needed. They worried about lawsuits.

Chartreuse, on the other hand, was shopping the universe for a brave new business in which to invest. She took a leap of faith on us and for that I am grateful, even though she can be a micro-manager at times. Basically, she owns our souls during the critical first stage of The Hope Store's infancy. Three months. About the time it takes for a peace lily to open its single white blossom in indirect sunlight. About the time that Amanda's Attic lets you keep a piece of furniture on layaway before putting it back in stock. To succeed at our goal, we need to earn enough capital to cover the sizable startup costs...and make a formidable profit.

Moving with great intent, I see a handsome man with tousled ginger hair and beard make his way through the opening night crowd. Imagine Prince Harry a decade older and a bit less giddy. It's none other than left-leaning Andrew Konstant from

CNN. His blue eyes have been said to hypnotize his interview subjects into telling all. He's a rising star on CNN covering international news and quirky science segments. The crowd parts for him in a Red-Sea-like fashion. He raises a microphone to his lips. "Could I have a word with you, Mr. Nagano?" he says in his gentle voice. "Andrew Konstant from CNN." We shake hands.

"I watch you almost every night," I say. I offer him a glass of champagne but Andrew waves it off, professional that he is. He is working after all. And with that, a bright light snaps on and the reporter thrusts a microphone into my face. "Actually, I'm a fan of yours," I say.

"Flattery will get you everywhere," he says. "But seriously, the person I first want to talk with is your partner Kazu Mori. I have some technical questions for him."

I wave over my better half. The cameraman comes in closer. "Allow me to introduce you to the smartest man in the room," I say. Andrew and Kazu shake hands.

"Kazu," he begins, "The world is dying to know exactly what makes The Hope Store tick. I'm positively fascinated. How is it exactly that you create hope here at The Hope Store?"

"That's an excellent question, Andrew," says Kazu. "But the answer to your question cannot simply be told in words. It must be experienced. Does that make sense?" The bartender starts making a racket with the blender. He's busy creating some foofoo drink.

"Let's start simple then. Does the hope come in the form of a pill or a procedure? Is the remedy psychological, biological, or divine? The press release played it pretty coy." Andrew holds the mic before Kazu, but Kazu is speechless. Is he panicking? He's less used to dealing with the media than I am.

I decide to chime in. "I'd say our remedy is pretty divine. But then I'm hardly objective." I giggle at my own joke. Andrew remains stone-faced. "It's a joke, Andrew! It doesn't cost more to laugh now and then." The reporter gives a half-smile.

"But you didn't answer my question. Is there some divine, otherworldly element involved?"

"All will be revealed soon enough," I say.

"That's not an answer," says Andrew.

"Not all questions have answers," I continue. "Not all answers can be put into words."

The reporter squints. "That's not an answer. That's a fortune cookie." Andrew laughs, then catches himself. "Oh, I didn't say that because you guys are Asian American."

Kazu jumps in. "We really appreciate public television's interest in The Hope Store, Andrew. I'm sorry we can't tell you more right now. But I promise you that the answers our store provides...will be well worth waiting for."

And with that, Andrew sighs heavily and turns away from his tight-lipped interviewees. He looks straight into the camera. "Well, I wanted to get The Hope Store creators to shed some light on the technology behind the hope installation process, but as you can see -- for whatever reason, they're choosing not to share that. This is my takeaway. They wouldn't confirm that there is a miraculous element to The Hope Store. But, more importantly, they wouldn't deny it either." He does not exactly wink into the camera, but he comes pretty close. "This is Andrew Konstant at the opening of The Hope Store in Chicago." The TV lights click off.

"I'm serious, guys," Andrew says. "You have to dig a little deeper and give me a better scoop or my producer might nix this segment completely. CNN does not do puff pieces."

Kazu and I simply nod and smile. Smile and nod. What else can we do? When I glance back at Andrew, I notice the reporter is planted at the bar, reaching for a glass of something yummy and dangerous looking. So much for professionalism. It is as if the reporter is rallying himself for a challenging night. As if he is off the clock, instead of on it.

Kazu goes to see how things are going at the front desk. I slip away to get a large coffee urn that's packed away in the second-floor storage room. At least that's what I will tell anyone who asks where I went.

But the truth is: I am up to something..

JADA

11. A PARALLEL WORLD

I make my way to the press opening for The Hope Store knowing I'm not press and that my name will not be found on the guest list. No amount of hoping will change that. If all else fails, I can pull out my trump card: that I actually took a class from Kazu ten years ago. But what if he doesn't remember me and I totally embarrass myself? Wouldn't be the first time. The party is in full swing when I arrive fashionably late...dressed in a sparkly black cocktail dress with silver hoop earrings big enough to shoot basketballs through. I've never actually crashed a party before in my life, but this is no ordinary party.

It's an exorcism for the hopeless and the helpless. And the fine journalists who write about them.

With a couple of butterflies in my stomach, I approach the check-in table. There is Kazu Mori. He hasn't aged a bit. Damn those good Asian genes. When I took his class I was a shy girl who never opened her mouth, except to catch the occasional fly. He looks up at me but shows no sign of recognition. That's just fine with me. I have no good news to share on my past decade. I have not found the cure for cancer or gained access to the parallel world.

"Good evening and welcome to The Hope Store," he says smiling. "I am Kazu. May I have your name please so I can check you in?"

I smile. "Of course. It's Upshaw. Jada Upshaw." My name doesn't seem to ring a bell with him either. *What am I? Chopped liver?* Kazu looks dashing in his purple dress shirt with the golden fish swimming across it. His longish black hair is curled behind his ears. Kazu's face is very Japanese and very kind, just as I remember it. He scans the Excel spreadsheet earnestly.

"I love how you guys have decorated the place!" I exclaim, my eyes drawn to the dramatic waterfall in the center of the store. I don't know how a thing can be dramatic and relaxing at the same time, but it is.

Kazu looks up, with puzzlement on his face. "That's funny. I don't see your name on the sheet. Did you RSVP?" He takes a sip of his champagne.

"Dang. I thought I did, but I can't swear to it," I say. "I've been so spacey this week!"

"I wish I could let you in, but we're filled to capacity. Who did you say you write for?"

"I didn't," I say. *He's going to make me go there.* I look deep into his eyes and smile. "Kazu, you really don't remember me? I'm going to be very hurt."

"Have we met before?" It is now his turn to look deep into my eyes.

"Ten years ago you taught a class at the Learning Annex. On parallel worlds. I was your student," I say.

"Parallel worlds," he says slowly. Kazu's eyes look sideways as he searches his memory banks. "What a fascinating topic."

Oh, shoot. Could I have the wrong Kazu Mori? I'm starting to feel embarrassed. I'd be turning red about now if I weren't black.

"I don't think that is possible," he says with utter politeness. "I didn't live in Chicago ten years ago."

"Oh my," I say, rubbing my warm forehead. "This is truly embarrassing." The awkward moment just hangs there as the two of us stand in suspended animation.

"Gotcha!" he shouts and lets out a gleeful, childlike laugh. "As soon as you walked in, I thought you looked familiar."

"You remembered me?" I ask.

"Then I saw your name and I knew it had to be you, the young woman from my parallel worlds class. I was pulling your leg," Kazu says.

"I wouldn't blame you if you couldn't remember me. I'm not the most memorable woman to walk this earth," I say.

"You're not going to believe this, but I still remember the paper you wrote in class!"

"You do not. Now I know you're teasing me."

"I'm serious," he says. "Your take on parallel worlds…it was so unique, so moving. What was the title? It was catchy. Something about…what you'd be doing, uh, it was, oh shoot, don't tell me…"

"I don't think I even remember the title," I say.

Then his Japanese eyes light up. "IN A PARALLEL WORLD, I'M PERFECTLY NORMAL. That was your title. It a was funny paper too."

Was I ever funny? Perhaps in a parallel world, I have a sense of humor. "Oh my god! I think that *was* the title. It certainly sounds like something I'd write. Does this mean you'll let me into the party?"

"I insist you come as my personal guest," he says. I see there is a line of people behind me waiting to be checked in. Kazu is writing something on a business card. "Here's my personal cell number. We have to catch up. Ten years is a long time. I can't wait."

"But I guarantee you that I haven't done --"

I hear a man clear his throat behind me. "Excuse me. I don't mean to interrupt this happy reunion," he says, "but if you could check me in, that would be great. I've already kept a good friend waiting --"

"Not a problem. Sorry," says Kazu to the man. Then he says to me, "Please call me so we can catch up." He hands me a press kit and off I go. I'm still in shock that he remembered me from all those years ago, even remembered the title of my paper!

I mill about the crowd for I am on a fact-finding mission. I want to eavesdrop on conversations, soak up the flavor, but I don't want to draw attention to myself. I comb through the press folder for some answers. The press release says: "The actual hope installation takes just five minutes, but the benefits of new-found hope last about a year. Annual booster installations are recommended. Three years of clinical studies have proven the hope procedure is safe and effective at increasing hope levels." But how do they create the damn new hope supply in the first place? That's what we are all dying to find out.

In one corner of the store, I spy a cluster of giddy, black women my age having a good laugh. I drift over toward them. One woman is holding court: "So I said to my husband, if they're giving away samples of hope in little trial-size bottles – I'd be sure to nab a handful of them to bring home for our whole, hope-challenged family!" And all the women laugh so hard their eyes are watering.

"Stop, Valerie!" says a woman with her hair swept out to the side and tied with a powder blue ribbon. It's a smart look on her. "You're making my mascara run. If we keep carrying on like this, they're going to toss us out of this place and repossess our goodie bags!" Valerie laughs along with them. I pretend-laugh to ease my way into the group.

I turn to the woman with the blue ribbon in her hair. "Are they really giving away free samples of hope tonight?"

"That's the rumor," she says. "But then, I think I'm the one that started the rumor." Both women laugh.

"I'm Jada, by the way," I say. Everyone smiles and nods. "Does anybody have any idea how the hope installation process actually works?"

"I'll give it a shot," says the blue ribbon. "They introduce a magnetic field around your brain. That's supposed to somehow trick your brain into creating more dopamine. More dopamine equals more hope? Something like that," the woman says. "I'm Natalie by the way." We shake hands. The other women start to drift off toward the food line.

"So Natalie, would you ever get an extra dose of hope, or do you think that's messing with Mother Nature?"

"I had a facelift. Why not a hope lift?" Natalie's statement is as serious as a heart attack.

A handsome guy with a microphone in hand sails through the crowd. It's that guy from cable. Andrew *something*. He shakes Luke's hand and starts to interview him. I gently crisscross my way through the crowd so I can get closer. Everyone in the store is gathering round to hear what they are saying. Except for the barista who is making some kind of slushy coffee drink. His blender grinds the ice, making a godawful sound.

Andrew begins: "Good evening, everyone. Let's start very simply. Does the hope installation come in the form of...*B-R-R-R-R...* psychological, biological, or divine? The press release says that...*B-R-R-R-R.*"

Andrew gives a look to the cameraman who in turn gives a look to the barista. The camera dude exchanges a few words with the man at the bar who nods apologetically.

Andrew starts again. "We're at the opening night of a very special store, the first of its kind in the world. They call it THE HOPE STORE."

The camera swings over to Luke and Kazu. They smile, raising their glasses of champagne in a toast.

"So what exactly is a Hope Store, and why should we care? What does it promise to do that's so groundbreaking? And I should mention I'm talking with the creators of said Hope Store -- Luke Nagano and Kazu Mori."

Luke leans into the microphone. "First of all, I'd like to say how thrilled we are that CNN is here tonight. Now to answer your question, Andrew, The Hope Store is the first store in the world that sells hope over the counter. Because of a brilliant new procedure pioneered by my partner Kazu Mori here...for the first time we offer a way to install hope in the hope-impaired masses."

"Kazu Mori, wunderkind of the science world," says Andrew. "How exactly do you install hope in a human devoid of hope? This is not a pharmaceutical drug, right?"

"No, it's not a drug at all," says Kazu.

"And it's not a surgical operation, right?"

"It's an out-patient procedure and not very invasive at all," says Kazu Mori.

"Okay, throw us a few bones here. Is it bigger than a breadbox?"

Kazu smiles. "Allow me to use some visual aids." Luke holds up a model of the brain. "This is the human brain, the most astonishing organ known to man. It stores our memories, interprets our life experiences, determines if we are happy or sad."

"Yes, I think I have one of those," says Andrew.

"I'm sure you do. And a very smart one too," says Luke.

Kazu carries on: "But as sophisticated as this device is, it's also fallible. I've devoted my life to learning how we can trick the brain into creating more dopamine, which is the neurotransmitter which empowers us to have hope. We've known for decades that dopamine and hope were linked, but for the first time we now have a way to put that knowledge into great use and help people lead more productive lives.

Luke jumps in: "We like to say it's both revolutionary and evolutionary. In short, it's a very big deal."

"Okay, you've got my attention," says Andrew. "How much is this hope procedure going to set me back, and does insurance cover it?"

"The price for a hope installation is just $750, down from the regular price of $1,000. We are currently in talks with insurance companies to show them how covering this procedure can save them money in the long run."

The reporter studies the back of his right hand. "Look at me. I'm getting goosebumps on national TV." He holds his hand up to the camera. The cameraman gets a close-up shot. He looks straight into the camera. "Well, I wanted to get the store creators to shed some light on the technology behind The Hope Store. I got that and more. It seems it all comes down to some ground-breaking neurological... brain tricks." The anchor winks into the camera. "This is Andrew Konstant for CNN coming to you live from The Hope Store in Chicago."

The feeling in this store is electric. It seems that everyone wants to sign up for a hope installation to see what it can do for them. There is a flurry of questions. *When can I get an appointment? Are there any side effects? Does it work for people with pre-existing conditions? Are hopelessness and depression considered two separate animals?*

These are just a few of the questions I overhear tonight. The party seems to be shifting into a higher gear and I feel a headache coming on. I grab a few pieces of sushi from the table and roll them into a napkin and head out the door. I have learned as much as I'm going to learn for one night. If I learn any more, my head just might explode. Tonight these guys are the hottest thing since sliced bread. Or they're the most clever charlatans on the planet. Time will tell. I can't want to debrief with Otis.

⋅ ★ ⋅

At home, I make myself some hot chocolate. I heat the saucepan with milk and pour in some Hershey's real chocolate syrup. My cat Shadow rubs up against the legs of my pajamas. She's happy to see me. She keeps me company as I sip my chocolate and think about tomorrow.

It was great to see Kazu. If I call him, he'll want to grab coffee and then he will discover how I've wasted the past ten years of my existence. He will try to be very encouraging because that's Kazu, but inside he'll feel sorry for me, and I'll leave feeling awful. And if we meet for coffee, I know I'll try to pump him for information about The Hope Store since he is its creator. I will feel like I am using him, which I will be. And that will feel crummy too.

There has been a lot of hoopla tonight. I predict The Hope Store will either be a gigantic flop along the lines of the Edsel, or the store is going to win every prize known to mankind. All I ever won in my life was first place in a dumb science fair.

And in this exact moment I decide I'm going to do it. I'm going to get me some of that hope juice.

It will be my own secret science fair project. And I will prove to the world that The Hope Store is an epic fail, fool's gold, snake oil for suckers. Maybe I'll call up that freelancer guy from the café to write an exposé on the Hopeless Store. It will be my revenge on those damned makers of all those miracle cures that never saved me from nothin'. What was that weird guy's name, uh, uh, it was a funny name, something *Matters*. I think I still have his card somewhere.

I'll put the hefty fee on my credit card and pray it doesn't get declined, and with any luck I'll have successfully suicided before the bill arrives. I go to my laptop and visit The Hope Store website. I send an email saying that I would like to make an appointment for 9 a.m. sharp. Good thing I'm in bed early. I set my alarm clock. I lie in bed and shut my eyes, but I don't sleep. I never sleep. I haven't slept in years.

LUKE

12. SHAME ON YOU

Once again Andrew Konstant steps into the bright lights holding his microphone like it is the Torch of Truth. Everyone at the party is a bit star-struck to see him. He looks into the camera with all the swarthy good looks his parents have given him and speaks: "We're back. I'm reporting from the opening night for The Hope Store, the first store in the world that claims to sell hope over the counter. Joining me are the store's creators Kazu Mori and Luke Nagano. First of all, let me say congratulations again on this momentous occasion. I know you two have been working on this for some years. This is your baby, as it were."

Our eyes adjust to the camera lights and there is Andrew with his disarming smile. "Thank you, Andrew. Yes, this is our baby and we are its proud fathers."

Andrew continues to probe. "For The Hope Store to offer some kind of artificial hope in an era where real hope is in such short supply is nothing short of brilliant. I give you that. I do." Andrew hasn't blinked and I wonder if that is something he learned in broadcasting school. Never let them see you blink. "But of course, and pardon me for saying so, but if The Hope Store fails to deliver, or if it's some kind of scam – then shame on you. Dr. Trenton Kohler, Director of Biotechnology at the University of Chicago goes as far as to accuse The Hope Store of taking advantage of the hopeless and profiting from their suffering. Care to comment?"

I take a swig of champagne and swallow slowly, attempting not to feel defensive. "Andrew, you're absolutely right. If we were getting people's hopes up for nothing -- that would be cruel. It'd also make for a terrible business plan." I laugh, but Andrew remains poker-faced. "As for exploiting the hopeless, the benefits of the treatment will speak for themselves. I can only say that Kazu and I know first-hand the devastating effect of hopelessness. Over the years, we've lost some very dear friends and family to suicide. If The Hope Store can give even a tiny ray of hope to the hopeless – we will have succeeded."

Kazu adds, "We firmly believe we've stumbled onto the real thing, and we can't wait for the world to find out just how real it is."

"So can you tell us more about how the hope process works?" says Andrew.

Kazu and I trade glances. "We also believe that the less one knows about how the procedure works – the more effective it is," I say. "Kazu and I agree that you just have to experience a hope installation for yourself. If anyone wants to take the plunge, go to our website…TheHopeStore.com and schedule an appointment. We're very excited to begin our work here in Chicago."

Overall, Kazu and I are pleased with how the event is going. Technically April is supposed to be managing things. She is the office manager after all, but the only thing she's managing to do at the moment is flirt with a hunky catering dude, the one in the tuxedo with the faux hawk. She is one of those people who was born without boundaries, a gypsy of a gal. At one point, I note we are running out of champagne and ask April to run over to Binney's. She says, "This is The Hope Store. Why don't you just *hope* for more champagne?"

"Because, sweet April, we don't believe in wasting our hope on tasks that we can just as easily delegate to you." She sticks out her tongue at me playfully and goes on her errand.

As my eyes scan the store, I note several of the local media have arrived. I need to circulate. I approach Madeline Worth of the Chicago Tribune. "Madeline, I'm so glad you could make it tonight. I know you had a conflict with the Steppenwolf opening."

"Mr. Nagano, I presume?" I nod. She is a bright woman who got canned from one paper for getting too frisky with an interviewee. They're married now. *When does an interview become a date?* I look around the room but all I see are Tsunami waves and earrings.

Madeline takes a bite of an hors d'oevre constructed out of a sliver of sourdough bread and goat cheese studded with pistachio nuts. "So what are we actually going to see tonight, and when are we going to see it? I'm a very busy woman. I still might try to catch the second act over at Steppenwolf if there's time."

"Well, my partner Kazu and I will talk a little. And then we'll give a tour of the premises."

"Is Kazu your lover? If so, you make an adorable couple." Madeline has never been known for her subtlety.

"I prefer the term partner. Lover sounds like all we do is lie in bed making love and eating grapes. Which is of course exactly what we do, but that's no one's business but our own." I flash a smile. "Excuse me, Madeline. I see NPR is here --"

"Whatever you do," she said, her lips dusted in goat cheese crumbles, "please do it in the next fifteen minutes. It will be intermission soon!"

By evening's end, Kazu and I are exhausted. Kazu says his face hurts from smiling so much. We stand by the door thanking our guests for coming. As people spill out onto the sidewalk, there is suddenly an odd sound. Wild, laughing-in-church kind of laughter. Kazu and I go outside to see what the commotion is about. Guests are pointing up at the store sign. The sign now reads:

THE HYPE STORE

A sheet of paper containing the letter "Y" has been strategically taped over the "O" in our sign.

Photographers are taking pictures. Kazu is mortified. And that is when Andrew and his public television crew emerge from the store. "I just hope that Andrew doesn't look up," I say to Kazu. But of course, Andrew looks up. His cameraman swings around to get a wide shot.

In a jovial voice, Kazu announces: "Looks like we have some young hoodlums in the neighborhood. Perhaps if they had a little more hope, and a little less beer -- they might find a more constructive use of their talents." The crowd is laughing with him.

Still I know it is possible that images of this vandalism could wind up in print or online tomorrow. I approach Andrew. "You aren't going to use that footage of the sign, are you?"

He smiles. "I'll have to see how it all works out in the final edit. I think we got some good stuff tonight."

"Yes, I think you did some fine reporting, Andrew. I'd just hate for the word 'hype' to be associated in any way with our store."

"Don't worry. It was great meeting both of you. Good luck on the store. Seriously."

I reach out to shake his hand. "My pleasure. Let me give you my card, in case you have any questions." In one sweeping motion, I pluck my business card out of a pocket and tuck it into the pocket of Andrew's sport coat. And with this simple gesture – the two of us have become inextricably linked.

·✦·

When we finally get home Kazu and I head straight to bed, for tomorrow we will open the store to our first customers. In bed in the half-dark, we exchange our last few words.

"Who do you think could have messed with our sign? Do we have any enemies you know about?" Kazu asks.

"None that I can think of. What about your fellow scientists? Do you think anyone of your colleagues might be jealous that The Hope Store could be a hit?"

He laughs. "I won't name any names, but there are plenty of competitive, jealous and fairly unstable personalities who work in America's laboratories. There are good folks too, but lots of characters." I smile at his candor. "The thing is, it would have to be someone who would be able to get to the sign. Someone had to use a very tall ladder from the sidewalk, or maybe they messed with the sign from the second floor."

"Yeah, all the tenants in the building have access to the second floor for storage," I say. "I wonder if there are any tenants who don't want us in the building." I lean over and turn on my sleep machine which plays the sound of falling rain in a Brazilian rain forest. As I lie in bed, I am aware this is not the first time I have kept a secret from my partner.

There is one big secret I've kept from Kazu that I worry will catch up with me one day. It's about how I came to know Kazu. When we met at LiveWell Labs, I learned that my response to the hope installation was average. I could see my days in the clinical trial were numbered. Surely Kazu would find me infinitely more interesting if I was a Super Responder, someone whose hope response was breathtaking.

I wanted Kazu to find me breathtaking too. So I faked my super response.

Some nights I fear I will start talking in my sleep and confess all my sins. If that ever happens, I'm in trouble big time.

Kazu and I lie in comfortable silence in our man-sized bed, assembled lovingly according to the IKEA instructions. We are horizontal in bed with only the light of the moon pouring in through the window. I think of the decades that preceded Kazu when I was single, wondering if I'd ever settle down with a life partner. I didn't think I was capable of having a long-term anything. Those were my days of no hope. Then I met Kazu and now look at me. Look at how easy it is. It's mystical and mysterious, love is. It happens when it happens. As my microscope-gazing hubby says: Energy can neither be created nor destroyed. It can only change forms. And what is love if not energy?

See how this works? Tip a man over and all his secrets pour out.

No rest for the wicked. One soft opening down. One public opening to go. Monday is just days away.

JADA

13. IMPORTANT MEETINGS

God, what time is it? I wonder. 2 a.m. It's a time when lovers are cuddling and rapists are raping and insomniacs like me are studying the cracks in the ceiling the way palm readers study the lines in a hand. Is there a future up there for me, or just cracked plaster? It's times like this I'm glad Otis doesn't live with me. Why ruin someone else's sleep just because mine is ruined? Adding to my usual insomnia is my sense of anticipation that I am going to get my hope installation tomorrow. I know Kazu Mori is a smart man, but the idea of a hope store still sounds like science fiction to me, like those sea monkeys they used to advertise in the back pages of comic books.

And now I'm thinking again about the freelance dude I met at Rendezvous. Blair Matters. I get out of bed and turn on a lamp, start looking through my purse, scanning the surface of my desk. There it is: his business card. I see it lists Blair's email as well as phone number. What the heck. I'm not falling asleep anytime soon. I turn on my laptop and start composing an email:

Dear Mr. Matters,

You probably didn't expect to hear from me. Or maybe you did. I met you recently at Rendezvous Café. You were good enough to keep an eye on the cute little mischief-makers I was babysitting. And you gave me your card. To be honest, I have never needed a freelance writer in my life. Until this week.

Please let me know if you could meet me soon at the café to talk about a possible project that may be of interest to you. I have googled you and see that you have some expertise in writing consumer protection pieces.

Jada Upshaw

I hope I won't regret it, but I give him my cell number too. I place Blair's card into my wallet. I turn off the lamp and climb back into bed. I've been on unemployment now for two years and it's about to run out. I keep getting foreclosure notices for the tiny, over-priced condo I call home...so I suspect that means my next stop is the streets of the Windy City. Yikes. And what little money I make under the table by transcribing the therapy sessions of the chronically hopeless? That goes straight to cigarettes and coffee. Now someone in the unit above me is walking around in high-heeled shoes. Who does that at 2 a.m. except maybe a hooker? I poke the ceiling a few times with a broom handle and wonder if that's where the cracks come from.

Most people don't know about my endless weekends when the only human contact I have is the Domino's delivery guy. Or nights like this when I try to fall asleep to the sounds of a life being lived one floor above me. *Oh, Miss High Heels, promenading back and forth. Do you think you're in some kind of fashion show? Maybe I should put on my high heels and promenade with you.*

There's nothing to really keep me here on planet earth. I've got no anchors. I try to be positive, to hope for things, only to get doors slammed in my face. If I ever manage to snag another job interview, I hope they ask me that awful question: "Where do you see yourself in five years?" I'll say: "I don't see myself anywhere in five years except six feet under." And I will take a picture of the interviewer's face with my cell phone, for that will surely be a Kodak moment.

My friend Simone is a shrink. I saw her a few weeks ago for coffee and she lent me a book that was filled with stories of transformation...individuals who changed into whole new people thanks to pills or therapy or sheer brute force. Each story reads like a fairy tale to me. My favorite one is about an older woman who is a widow. The woman is convinced that each night when she lies down to sleep, there is a man under her bed. The man mutters things she cannot understand at first. Then the woman's doctor prescribes Seroquel which is good for schizophrenia, bipolar disorder, mania, and a whole host of stuff. And low and behold, soon the woman comes to understand what the man is muttering. He is saying, "Did you lock the door?" These words terrify her. They are so personal, so threatening.

The next night the man under the bed says to her, "Would you like some hot chocolate?" This utterance is almost funny, but now she knows who the voice belongs to. These are the things her late husband used to say right before turning in for the night. After the meds fully kick in, the voices go away completely. She starts to miss the voices, but there is nothing the doctor can do to bring them back.

There are no pills to start the voices; only pills to stop them. Part of me wonders if a hope installation could have helped.

Later today I will look around my place for my art supplies. I will create a diorama of The Hope Store out of construction paper and glue, make little action figures of Luke and Kazu out of clay. Little voodoo dolls I can stick pins into if they fail to flood my brain with hope juice.

I remember back in fourth grade, I entered our school's science fair. My plan was to create a diorama of the Great Chicago Fire and show how the fire could have been prevented with the help of science, or at least how the fire could have been contained. I managed to dig up a stray shoe box in my mother's closet and pulled off the lid. I set the box on my desk so that the open side faced me.

How carefully I girl-handled those scissors to produce the paper silhouette of Mrs. O'Leary, her naughty cow that started the fire, and the oil lantern. I used little pieces of Cap'n Crunch Cereal to stand in for bales of hay in the barn. My teacher Mr. Epstein thought it was brilliant. But my favorite part was the fire itself, of course. The fire was conjured out of a combination of shreds of orange and red tinfoil, black construction paper, and sprinkles of gold glitter. When the judges saw the finished product, they were speechless. The fire looked alive, combustible, beautiful. They had no choice but to give me first place.

Many years later, Mr. Epstein told me that the judges secretly found the diorama disturbing. They worried that it somehow celebrated the fire itself, instead of bringing focus to the importance of good fire prevention habits. But how do you tell that to a nine-year-old girl without discouraging her? They didn't say a word to me that day. The judge leaned over and pinned that blue satin ribbon to my sweater, and the students in the auditorium actually clapped for me that day. No one has ever clapped for me like that again.

I turn the lamp back on and start to search through my closets. There must be an empty shoe box in here somewhere. When am I going to organize my closets? One thing is clear to me: I am not getting to sleep tonight.

I am at Rendezvous Café sitting at my regular table drinking an Italian soda with mint Torani syrup. The emerald green beverage looks amazing, the ice cubes which bob below the surface resemble floating jewels. Blair Matters strolls in.

"Thanks for making time to meet with me on such short notice," I say.

"I'm happy to do it. I knew you couldn't stay away from me forever." His flirtatious manner is off-putting, but right now I need his services more than I need his good behavior. "How can I help?" he says.

Blair takes a seat across from me, tossing his messenger bag to the floor.

I start my pitch, choosing my words carefully. "Remember you said I should keep your card in case I ever needed a freelancer?" He smiles. "Well, I think I need a freelancer. Have you ever heard of something called The Hope Store?"

Blair's eyes widen. "Have I ever. They've been on my radar since clinicals started some years ago."

I take a gulp of my drink. "So do you think it's really possible to install man-made hope into people? It sounds kind of crazy to me."

"I'll go you one better and say it sounds dangerous." He pulls out a small notepad and starts taking notes. "So where do I come in?"

"This might seem a little...*strange*..."

"I like strange. Strange is good."

"I want you to help me prove that The Hope Store is a scam. Blair, I've been hopeless my whole life and experts have tried to hypnotize me, electric-shock me, medicate me, meditate me, I've tried holistic and I've tried the holy ghost. I'm telling you none of these things has ever given me one single day of hopefulness. I'm sure The Hope Store is no different." I look at Blair to see if he's with me or not.

"Go on."

"So I plan to be a guinea pig and get a hope installation. And then when nothing happens, I want you to write about that nothingness, my misadventures at The Hope Store. I don't want any other poor, hopeless people to waste their money on snake oil.

"What will you pay me to write this piece?"

"Wouldn't the magazine or newspaper pay a fee? I don't know how these things work," I say.

Blair rubs his chin. "I used to be an up-and-comer in this town. I did exposés that protected consumers. I slew some dragons in my day. But one of my stories blew up in my face and I lost my confidence."

"What happened? If you don't mind my asking."

"I don't really want to go into it. But long story short: I was writing an article about a colleague of mine. She was moving money around at the company where she was CFO. I felt some conflict since she was a friend, but I had my facts straight and the paper ran the story. The next day, she jumped into the Chicago River and drowned."

"That's terrible. But that was her choice; not yours. No one can know what goes through the mind of a person who wants to take their life," I say. "You can't blame yourself."

"But I did blame myself," Blair says. There is a vulnerability in his face that I didn't think was inside him. "And even when I stopped blaming myself, there were plenty of other people who were happy to blame me. But I think it could be my time again, to write that big story. You have yourself a partner." We shake hands.

I take another sip of my emerald green potion. Blair looks out the coffeehouse window.

"I think this is a really important article," I say. "And I think it could be a great story for your comeback. You could…redeem yourself, not that you need to. What do you say"

"Jada, you had me at *strange*." He walks to the counter and gets himself some black coffee and a scone big enough to prop open a heavy door.

"Tomorrow, the store opens to the public," I say. "I'll be there. We'll be in touch." I rise from the table. Blair Matters looks like he's going to stay.

"Jada, I don't think you know what this means to me, but thank you. I'm looking forward to working with you." I wave to him as I leave the café. I join the stream of pedestrians on Clark Street on their way to important meetings of their own.

JADA

14. SMALL HUMANS

I make my way to Sheila's house to babysit her kids again. At least we'll be at her house this time and not in a public place. Tomorrow is Halloween. My sister really gets into the holidays. Her front lawn looks like a graveyard with bandaged mummies doing sit-ups in their coffins. Charming. There are illuminated jack-o-lanterns on every flat surface in her house. Willis is playing a shoot-em-up game on the computer.

Angie comes running up to me dragging a shopping bag behind her. "Mommy said you could help me try on my costume, Aunt Jada."

"She did, did she?" I open up the bag and pull out the contents. It's an astronaut costume.

"Isn't it beautiful?" she says.

"Well, looks like someone wants to get lost in space. Would that be you, Angie?"

She nods her head eagerly. "I want to explore things and find the other people. There must be life on other planets, don't you think?"

I want to tell her that I'm not even sure there is life on earth, but I hold my sardonic tongue.

"I want to tell you a secret, Angie," I say but I remember how Sheila likes to sugarcoat things. I'm not to tell any hard truths to the kids.

WHAT I REALLY WANT TO SAY TO MY NIECE IS: "Angie, when you grow up you're going realize that the happiest days of your life were these stupid days right now...because no one expects anything from you. That the dreams you have of growing to be an astronaut or the president or a princess -- they ain't gonna happen. Instead, you'll slave away at a job you're terrified of losing and even more terrified of keeping. And when you retire, they'll give you a gold watch and a gift certificate to Walmart. Life will really get interesting as you try to survive on social security."

But I can't say that. So instead I say: "When you grow up, you're going be a lot older than you are now, and hopefully a lot wiser than I am."

"Come on, Aunt Jada," says Angie. "You were going to tell me a secret."

"She wasn't going to tell us a secret," Willis snaps at her. "She was going to give us some bad news."

And suddenly I don't know what to say. I don't want to depress the hell out of them. I look into the faces of Willis and Angie and they're so pure. They're not monsters. I am flooded with emotion for some reason.

Willis speaks. "Are you crying, Aunt Jada?"

"I'm fine, Willis." So instead of telling the complete truth, I say this: "Did I ever tell you how much I like your name, Willis?" He shakes his head no. "Your name Willis means you are a "protector." And Angie, you name means "angel or messenger."

They both are surprised.

"I like both of your names. And I like both of you," I say and I notice that Angie is crying.

"Angie, what's wrong, sweetie?" But she won't answer. She just cries harder. As if she had a premonition of her own future life. "We'll try on your costumes later. Let's eat dinner, kids. I'm treating for pizza."

I don't know how parents do it.

I don't know how they raise small humans to grow up to be large ones.

RESURRECTION

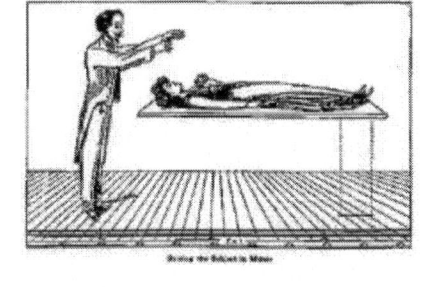

"But when I pass a magic wand over the subject's head,
what does she wish for? *Spiritual advancement*, she says.
To witness something, like a miracle or something."

-- from the poem "The Pursuit of Happiness"

LUKE

15. OUR PUBLIC AWAITS US

Today the store opens to the general public. I awake first at the unholy hour of 5 a.m. I gently turn off the alarm to prevent the scream of the clock. For a few moments I just lie in bed, thinking about what this day means to us, what this store means. And why success is so crucial to us.

For me, the failure of the store would mean going back to a day job that is soul-crushing at worst and distracting at best -- assuming I could even find an office-slave job in this economy. Back to wearing monkey suits for the entertainment of others, with neckties that always feel like nooses, no matter how loose they are. Worst of all, it would mean no longer working at The Hope Store. A place I will surely love working at.

For Kazu, it would mean something else. It would mean a very public, very epic fail for someone who is not used to failing, someone that is already on the radar of the science world. It would mean rubbing elbows with his peers at bio-tech symposiums as an also-ran, a laughing stock.

No, failure is not an option for either of us.

I am the first brave soul to stir from the warm bed. I log on to The Hope Store website. I'm tickled to see thirty or so emails from people wanting to make appointments. They've heard about the store from some Facebook ads we just started running. The emails are mostly from Chicago, but some are national. I'm especially excited to see that two are from the UK and three are from Japan! Wonderful.

It occurs to Luke that Madeline's review may be up on the Tribune website. I turn on the lamp near the bed and flip open my laptop. "I think the Tribune review might be up. Why don't you read it? I'm too nervous."

Kazu reads:

from the Culture Beat blog of the Chicago Tribune
"Hope Springs Eternal" by Madeline Worth

Last night, a new boutique put out its shingle in Chicago. It's called The Hope Store. The store claims to sell hope over the counter, and install it while you wait. Sounds like sci-fi but there may be reason for optimism. Will this be the biggest new business venture since Apple devoured the gadget market? Store creators Luke Nagano and Kazu Mori certainly hope so. But since the store just opened, it's too soon to tell what customer reaction will be. In this anemic economy we could all use a booster shot of hope.

Supposedly preliminary tests have been promising and the positive results have been duplicated, but I always feel these tests can be biased. The proof will be in the return customers. I'll follow the progress of The Hope Store and let all of my loyal readers know -- if it's an apple or a lemon.

I look at Kazu. "Hmm. I can't tell if that was a rave or a pan?" I say.

"That was a let's-wait-and-see," Kazu says. "She's going to withhold judgment until she sees what our profit margin is."

"We'll let you know if it's an apple or a lemon. I don't care for that snarky tone. With all the hors d'oeuvres that woman was wolfing down last night, she owed us a rave review."

"Actually I thought that line was pretty good," Kazu says. "Well, we better get up. We've got a big day ahead of us."

I turn on the TV to see if CNN has run the segment on us yet. I know it may not run for a day or two, but I can't resist checking anyway. Onscreen I see Andrew Konstant saying something about our store. Cool. "Kazu, the CNN segment is on!" Kazu slowly rouses himself, sits up in bed. As the camera pulls back, we see The Hope Store's ruined sign which reads: THE HYPE STORE.

"Oh, shit," Kazu and I both say at the same time.

Together we stare helplessly at the TV screen. Somehow in the course of the night,

Andrew's story has morphed, the whole angle has shifted. Instead of the segment celebrating our wondrous new store, Andrew is clearly is taking a devil's advocate approach.

The face of an Asian man with horn-rimmed glasses fills the screen. He is in his thirties and earnest-looking. His wears a gray pinstripe tie, no doubt to bolster his credibility. "Well, I have been following this so-called Hope Store ever since I first got wind of it about a year ago in the trades."

Andrew Konstant says, "So what do you think? Good idea, bad idea?"

The man smiles. "It's a horrible idea."

"Who is this bozo?" I say to Kazu.

The bozo continues: "I'm with a group called Natural Hopers United which is made up of consumer advocates and regular citizens who support wellness through natural means. Would you want some scientist poking around inside your brain? How do you even know it's safe?" On the screen, they give the man's name as "Robert Chang, Natural Hopers United."

Andrew replies, "Well in all fairness, the FDA says it's safe, so —"

"Yeah, and they've been wrong before, haven't they?"

"You have a point there, Mr. Chang," Andrew says. "So is your objection to artificially-created hope similar to the objection to steroids?"

"Exactly. These things give artificial advantages to a select few."

The news anchor smiles. "But by that token, we shouldn't allow anti-depressants or plastic surgery or cancer drugs. Shouldn't we want to be the best person that we can possibly be? Isn't that what evolution is? Isn't that our job as humans?"

Bozo the Clown has a pained look on his face. "We Natural Hopers would advocate for the banning all things that prevent the individual from discovering his or her own natural-born potential."

Andrew looks into the camera. "As you can see, not everyone is rolling out the red carpet for The Hope Store. But for those of you eager to get your hope on, The Hope Store opens to the public today at 9:00. This is Andrew Konstant, for CNN."

Kazu has been busily typing on his computer tablet during the broadcast. He says: "Natural Hopers United does not even come up in a Google search. Either they're very new, or they're very bogus."

My cell phone rings. It is an ungodly hour. "Hello?" I answer.

"Did you see it?" says the urgent voice of a woman.

"Chartreuse?"

"This is a disaster, Luke. How are you going to fix it?" she says. "We need some damage control pronto. Call me back with your action plan."

LUKE

16. EVIL SPIRITS

Traffic is heavy on Lakeshore Drive, so I choose to focus on the movement of the undulating waves of Lake Michigan. It soothes me. High on my agenda today is responding to lovely Chartreuse with a kick-ass PR strategy.

Kazu is the designated driver in the family as I never got the automotive gene. We are driving upstream going due north toward Andersonville, while most sane people are driving downtown to their respectable jobs. I had wanted to get to the store by 7:30 a.m. so we'd have plenty of time before we open at 9:00, but thanks to my chat with Chartreuse, it'll be closer to 8:00. I've got opening day jitters. As we approach the store, I'm surprised to see a cluster of about twenty-five people standing in line outside the store. Could they be customers? We welcome them and quickly learn that a few of them had read the article in the Tribune. Some saw the CNN story, but interestingly no one mentions the vandalized sign.

"We're going to see as many people as we can today," Kazu says to the group. "Just give us a chance to get settled in, and then we'll be opening our doors at nine."

Then I flash my husband a big, goofy grin. "Now, here's the most important question: Does anyone need some coffee?" I say. The crowd goes wild. "I'll take that as a yes. We're going to get a few kegs of Dunkin Donuts coffee for you folks. And maybe some Munchkins. See you shortly."

As we make our way into the store, Kazu mutters under his breath, "Donuts and coffee for the masses -- is that in our budget?"

"It is now." I smile. Kazu hurries ahead to open the door and we slip inside.

At the very front of the line stands a pretty black woman with a long graceful neck reading a book. She reminds me of a swan. "I guess I'm first," she says.

"Thanks for coming out today," I say.

✦

Kazu and I sit in the lunch room. He pours our coffees with extra cream and sugar. A playful sign on the far wall reads:

THIS LUNCH ROOM
IS A GOSSIP-FREE ZONE.

As if we had enough employees to start a rumor! I've made a conscious decision to remain calm this morning. After all, this is the first day the store opens to the general public and we must remain focused. I will respond to Chartreuse shortly. Everything will work out. I am *hopeful* of that.

"Obstacles arise when you move forward," Kazu says quoting one of his favorite Buddhist sayings to me. "This must mean we're moving forward." He winks at me to try to cheer me on. Luckily my hope levels are still high from my last installation in June. I can tell they're high because of the light that glimmers out of the corner of my eye from time to time. It's a glimmer unique to the hope installation. You can't look at this light directly no matter how hard you try; the more you try to look at it the more it moves away.

As for addressing the less-than-flattering coverage from the CNN story, I can start by reassuring Chartreuse using axioms I learned in marketing classes -- "Any press is good press." "As long as they spell our name right." -- but that will only take me so far. I need to plan and prioritize. Everything will need to be run past Chartreuse. Am I feeling stressed right now? Yes. Yes I am.

From where I'm seated, I don't have a direct view of the folks gathering outside the store so from time to time, I take a peek. That's me: I'm detail-oriented. Compulsively so. And somehow this makes me think of dear Chartreuse and what I need to do to appease her today. I make a plan of attack.

1. Draft an email to new prospects asking them to pay no attention to the scary man hiding

behind the curtain, that the Natural Hoper dude is just a science-hating tree hugger with too much time on his hands.

2. Have Kazu post the above text on the website and kiss me twice for good luck.

3. Tell Chartreuse it would be really great if she consented to having a hope installation of her own, as she is the only investor not to do so!!

Will this strategy control any damage from the CNN story? Hard to say. No one ever said that marketing and PR were exact sciences. All I know for sure is that this story will be played out over the next 24 hours. Kazu pours us more coffee because he believes there is no problem that cannot be solved by the proper mix of caffeine, cream and artificial sweeteners. I call back Chartreuse, putting her on speakerphone.

"That took long enough," barks Char, never one for gratuitous patience or empathy.

"And how are we doing this morning, Chartreuse?"

"Oh, I've been better. I'd be a lot better if I hadn't seen CNN's hatchet job. And the Tribune story was wishy-washy. So what've you got for me?"

"We've got lots of customers waiting in line at the store right now. Some saw the CNN clip and it didn't seem to bother anyone, so that's great." Kazu, who hates dealing with Chartreuse even more than I do, puts his hand over his ears to shield himself from peripheral abuse. "And we're getting some traction from the Facebook sidebars. Thirty people responded and asked for more info!"

"Just thirty? It should be 130 for what we're paying!" says the big mouth coming out of my tiny cell phone. I pick up my cell and take a peek at the crowd of customers. It seems to have grown.

"So I'm going to have April send out emails welcoming them and offering to book them for consultations," I say. "Kazu will help put some upbeat copy on our website's home page, something about how people tend to fear things that are unfamiliar and innovative." I look at Kazu and he gives me a thumbs-up. "And really, Chartreuse, since we're so new, any press we get helps to raise our profile."

Char's silence on the other end of the phone is deafening. "What are you going to say to the press?"

I look at Kazu. He shakes his head, expressing his wish for discretion.

"Hmm. I don't think it's a good idea to respond to the CNN story," I say. "I think if we leave the story alone, it will sink on its own weight. I really do."

"Well, I really don't. So whatever website copy you come up with, tailor it to the Trib, WBEZ, The Reader, CNN and the Sun-Times."

Kazu rolls his eyes for the both of us.

"Chartreuse, don't you think that by responding to the event, we're drawing attention to it?"

"I think that by *not* responding to the charges, we're saying the charges are true. I don't want to do that, Luke."

I can picture this woman's face shrivel into a prune the size of a human head. A prune wearing a snarky smile. I make a note per Char's instructions, but I have no intention of following up. I am planning to have a memory lapse later today. When I take a look at the crowd out front, I see something I don't expect: a handful of people carrying signs. The signs say: "NATURE IS THE REAL HOPE STORE." "NATURAL HOPERS UNITE!" "THE NOPE STORE." It looks like the Natural Hopers have found us. Of course, I mention none of this to Chartreuse.

"Please get our response on the website right now!"

"Of course. Kazu is –"

"And make sure you run all copy past me before releasing it," she says.

"Absolutely, Char."

"And don't call me Char." She hangs up.

Kazu makes the sign of the cross with his index fingers…to ward off evil spirits. Lot of good that'll do. I point to the tiny swarm of protestors moving in a circle on the sidewalk like gnats at a family picnic. Kazu rises and together we just stand there watching. "I think we have a situation on our hands, Husband," I say.

After huddling with Kazu over various options, we decide it's best to face our detractors head-on, before any reporters start appearing. The protestors continue to walk in a small circle in front of the store with their placards. I recognize the man who spoke on CNN for the Natural Hopers.

"Good morning," I say in a welcoming voice. His name escapes me. "I believe I saw you on CNN the other day. My name is Luke Nagano and this here is —"

"—I am well aware who you both are," he says. He ignores my offer to shake hands.

Kazu steps in. "We would be extremely interested to sit down with you over coffee to better understand your concerns with The Hope Store. Do you have time to get together this week? What day is best for you?"

"How about never?" The man just smiles at us through his horn-rimmed glasses.

I try again. "I know there is resistance in this country to finding answers to life challenges through medication and experimental treatments. These answers were once found mainly through spiritual paths or talk therapy or simple hard work. So along comes The Hope Store and we seem to offer big solutions with none of the effort, and that sounds lazy and wrong somehow." I am closely watching the man's face to gauge the impact of my words but he is poker-faced. I picture my words as beams of light, prying open a clenched fist. Ever since my first hope installation five years ago, my hopes have taken on a visual life of their own. "But I promise you that for a hope installation to really take hold, it requires a great deal of engagement and hard work from the individual. We'd love to be able to tell you more about it...if you have the time."

The Natural Hoper says with a smirk, "My concern with The Hope Store and its ilk goes beyond that fact that you seem to offer easy solutions to very big problems. One concern is that by giving your so-called hope installations -- and I have no idea how effective that treatment is or how safe it is – that you make it unnecessary for people to develop within themselves the ability to hope. Instead you make them dependent on purchasing your services indefinitely."

I look at Kazu to see if he wants to respond or I should. Kazu extends the palm of his hand toward me. "Well, I'm sorry, what is your name?" I say.

"Robert Chang."

"Robert, I love your concern that people might forgo developing in themselves the ability to hope," I say. "But surely you know that some people will never be able to hope on their own, no matter how hard they try, don't you?"

He hands me his business card. "This is what I acknowledge. I acknowledge that this conversation is way too important and way too complex to take place on a street corner in Andersonville. I'd like to suggest some kind of town hall meeting on the future of hope. You have my card. The ball is in your court. Good day for now." And the man begins walking north on Clark Street, followed by his colleagues with their placards in tow.

As the Natural Hopers clear out, I am stunned to see Chartreuse Johnson standing on the sidewalk in an olive trench coat. How did she get here so fast? I have no idea how much of this conversation she has heard, but I am sure it is way more than I would've liked.

"Wow, guys. Protesters at the opening day of The Hope Store? When were you going to share that one with me?" She gently sets a shopping bag down on the sidewalk.

"Chartreuse, I didn't expect to see you here today. And so quickly," I say.

"Well, when you called I was at the Starbucks next door. After I hung up, I was waiting for you to run web copy past me. Then I checked the site to see if you had updated anything. Finally, I decided to just drop in and see if you needed my...assistance." Char pauses and in this moment I see her gruff exterior soften. "Kazu, Luke, believe me, I do *not* want to micro-manage. So if you tell me everything is under control and I don't need to be here, I will turn around and take my butt over to my Pilates class. But I have invested far too much capital in The Hope Store to see it fail because of...carelessness."

I am surprised to hear Kazu speak first. "We really appreciate your investment and faith in the store, Chartreuse," he says. "I think everything that needs to happen today, it's stuff that only Luke and I can do. But I promise if we need your help, we will definitely call you."

Chartreuse picks up her shopping bag and hands it to me. "Here are flowers for the store. They're violet lotuses. Just fill up the glass bowl with water and let them float. They'll look stunning at the front desk. We'll meet at the end of the week."

I take a peek into the shopping bag. "They're beautiful, Chartreuse. Thank you," I say. "For everything."

When I get to my office, I sketch out some marketing ideas for November. Thanksgiving. Images of turkeys, cornucopias and gratitude dance through my head.

JADA

17. AUDITION

April opens the doors promptly at 9:00 a.m. She's a new hire to work the front desk and she's also a friend of mine. Kazu and I are dumbfounded to see that the protesters have scared away several customers. Somehow the Natural Hoper on CNN didn't stop customers from coming to our store, but a four-color pamphlet did. How weird is that? As I said before, marketing is an inexact science. Chartreuse is going to crucify me. Even though our dismal first day of business has nothing to do with the press coverage, I just know that somehow this is going to be my fault.

The lobby is almost empty. There are just a few brave souls sipping their Dunkin Donuts coffee, reading brochures. I make my way back to my office. I've just grabbed a fresh cup of coffee myself when April escorts the first customer to Kazu's office. From across the hall, I listen in. "Kazu Mori, it's my pleasure to introduce you to Jada Upshaw. Jada, this is —"

Without saying a word, Kazu and the customer collide in an intimate embrace.

"Oh, I see you've already met," she says, smiling. April pulls the door closed. When she sees me watching, she just shrugs her shoulders at me.

Kazu's office and my office have been intentionally designed so that our desks face each other. This way we can still feel connected, even when our client loads get heavy. Hopefully, we will miss each other less this way. After a few minutes, Kazu's door opens. I see him walk with his client toward my office. "Luke, I wanted to introduce you to someone, since this lovely human being is actually an old acquaintance of mine and our first customer."

"Any friend of Kazu's...I'm pleased to meet you and welcome to The Hope Store. We don't just instill hope --"

"--you install it. So I've heard. Catchy slogan," she says.

Kazu steps forward. "Since we're friends, I thought it would be more appropriate if I turn her over to you."

"Absolutely," I say. I remember her now. The pretty black woman who was first in line: the Swan Woman.

Kazu pulls the door closed after him.

Jada and I extend our hands toward each other. Beams of sunlight from my window cast a pattern on the floor between us, particles of dust dancing in the light. Our hands seem to take forever to reach each other. And finally, a handshake. Once two people have officially met, it cannot be undone.

Jada takes a seat on the blue sofa. The sound of April's giddy laugh can be heard through the door. I sit in an easy chair opposite her. I have an iPhone upon which to take notes.

"Well, Kazu's loss is my gain." She seems a bit nervous. I try to break the ice. "How do you and Kazu know each other?"

"Oh, it was a long time ago," she says. "Kazu was teaching a class at the Learning Annex. He's an excellent teacher."

"He is. He's thinking of holding seminars on hope enhancement at the store once things get settled. And we want to start a support group for Hopers Transitioning."

"Sign me up. I would like that." I allow more time for chit-chat before we get started. Jada just looks around my office, taking everything in. "I can't wait to see the hope contraption thingy," she finally says. I smile. Jada reaches into her purse. "Oh, those nutty protesters were handing out pamphlets. I got one for you guys." She hands it to me.

"Thanks!" I say.

The title on the front of the pamphlet reads: 10 REASONS TO BOYCOTT THE HOPE STORE. A quick glance reveals their manifesto. They present a list of low-cost strategies to increase one's hope naturally: health clubs to boost one's endorphins, cognitive therapy to correct flawed thinking, herbal remedies to enhance positive moods. The pamphlet gives a host of websites and services available as alternatives to our store. The brochure is no grassroots photocopy job. It is glossy, four-color printing on card stock. The Natural Hopers must have money. Someone has money.

But all I say to Jada is, "I'm sure it will make for lively bedtime reading tonight." I tuck the pamphlet into my bag. "Well, I'm happy to say you're my first client, Jada Upshaw. No pressure." She fidgets in her seat. "I can't tell you how grateful I am that you weren't scared off by the protesters."

"Oh," Jada says. "I had made up my mind I was going to get my installation. Those people didn't scare me."

"I know Kazu appreciates the support of an old friend," I say.

"It's nothing. So I'd like to talk about why I'm here today. Ever since I was young I knew I was different. I knew I was missing something."

"Absolutely. I think I know what you mean."

"People think I'm exaggerating when I say I haven't had a hopeful day in my whole life," she explain. "But who can speak to that better than me, right?"

"You have a point," I say.

"I've always been the quiet girl. The Disappearing Girl. But give me a chance to warm up, and I might actually come across as almost-lively," Jada says. "Though no one has ever outright accused me of being, uh, uh, what you call it when..." She is panicking. A word has escaped and she's got to find it. "...you know, when someone is..." There is a pause for a moment. A little sadness peeks out from behind her facade. She has failed.

"An extrovert?" I ask.

"That's it! *An extrovert.*" She sighs. "I used to have such a vocabulary, you wouldn't believe it. I used to win spelling bees in school. I don't know where those words have gone to...but I don't think they're coming back any time soon. Do you?"

"If they're important words, I think they come back to you. Tell me, Jada. What do you think hope is?"

"I never really thought about it. Hope is...believing things are going to get better. Believing that you're put here on this earth...for a reason. Most of all, hope is what other people have. That magic juice."

I jot a few notes in my tablet.

"So I guess this is my audition?" she asks.

"Audition? That's an interesting word. What do you mean?"

"When I first wanted to try anti-depressants, I told my doctor I felt like I was auditioning for Prozac. This where I'm supposed to sing for my supper, plead my case so I can be green-lighted for treatment, right?"

"Ah. Well, I'm not a doctor or a therapist --"

She continues: "I have tried medication, talk therapy, holistic remedies, self-help books, acupuncture and hypnosis. Nothing has helped. My depression is better, but my hopelessness is not. It hurts too much to try to hope anymore. I don't have it in me. So it's all on you, Luke, because I am dying here. I am disintegrating before your very eyes." For the first time I see the vulnerable woman sitting before me, a woman in unimaginable pain. I will do everything in my power to save her.

"Well then, what do you say we begin?" I rise from my chair. "Today, we'll do a brain scan of your current hope levels. Then I'll install your new hope. And tomorrow, I'll show you a short film about hope. Over the next four weeks, you'll get to experience your new hope levels firsthand. We'll have check-ins here every Friday. How does that sound?"

Jada rises from the sofa. "I have to tell you…" She stops.

"What?"

She looks up at me. "I don't know what I'm getting myself into."

I laugh. "There's something about the unknown that's a little bit scary, but a little bit irresistible too, don't you think?" I say. "But nothing will come up that you can't handle. I promise." I lead her toward the door. "And now I'll take you to the Installation Suite."

JADA

18. THE MAGNETIC MOMENT

Luke's manner is so damn comforting and kind that when he says, "Nothing will come up that you can't handle," I can't help but believe him, though my first impulse is to argue with him, throw myself to the floor kicking and screaming, tell him about all the times I've been led down roads like this only to be screwed over. But I decide to bite my tongue. Luke's voice is smooth and silky. I'm sure he missed his calling as a radio personality. There is a decorative water fountain on one corner of his desk. The water cascades endlessly over a small chunk of marble. Between the sound of the water and the sound of Luke's voice, I wonder if I am being hypnotized. And then I wonder if I care. No, not really. Anything is better than this imaginary life I am living. That I am *not* living.

Together, this Japanese American man and I walk down a corridor. As we walk further, I notice it starts to feel colder and the hallway gets darker.

Until finally we disappear.

"Luke?"

"Shh, we're almost there."

"Where? We're almost where?"

"Give me your hand. "Let me guide you a bit. We've almost reached the Installation Suite."

I give him my hand.

"I mean, it's not like I'm afraid of the dark, but, uh, uh…"

"I promise there'll be light soon," he says. "The darkness helps to separate your old life from your new one. We're wiping the slate clean. And we need to do a scan of you."

I stop walking for a moment. "What will you be scanning, pray tell?"

"Your brain."

I didn't see that one coming. Images from *The Bride of Frankenstein* flash through my mind, lightning bolts shooting through a beehive hairdo. "Wait, no one told me about this," I protest.

"It's perfectly safe. A regular MRI takes a picture of your body. A functional MRI kind of takes a snapshot of your brain activity and turns it into a pretty light show," he says. It feels warmer, the room grows brighter. Luke and I are restored. "It's a powerful record that you can take with you today. The before-and-after shots document changes in your hope capacity, and of course you'll have lots of anecdotal experiences. Shall we continue?"

I hesitate but I've come too far to turn back now. I can't wait to tell Blair Matters about all this science stuff mixed up with the new age stuff and to show him the protester pamphlet. I took some photos of the protest demonstration too.

"Will you let me know when we get to the actual hope installation?"

"Absolutely."

As we walk toward the Installation Suite, everything becomes warmer and brighter. The place looks exactly like a beauty parlor from the 1950s. The retro-style signs could have been stolen from beauty shops and barber shops of the past. The six adjustable chairs look vintage. I must admit the playful décor relaxes me. Good on them, the designer folks. Luke guides me to a seat.

"Is this going to hurt, Luke?"

"Not at all. It might tickle a bit. Just lean back against the headrest and hold as still as you can for about five minutes. And as you sit there, I want you to hope for something. And just keep hoping for that one specific thing as we wait for the picture to develop. Okay?"

"Okay, I guess."

Luke flips a switch. "Now hold still...and hope for something. Keep that one thing in your mind for the next five minutes." I hear the purr of a machine, a motor sound. It sounds much more intense than I expected. I close my eyes. I decide to hope for something unusual. I hope for lotus blossoms. In my mind's eye, I see...a clear glass bowl filled with purple lotus blossoms floating on water. It's not even something I want or like. But for the sake of the experiment, I will hope for it. It's not my birthday so I have a better chance being struck by lightning than receiving flowers.

"Are you hoping for something, Jada?" Luke asks?

"Yes, I am."

"Good. Just hold still for a few more minutes as I take the fMRI."

Finally Luke says I can relax. "Let me direct you now to the screen in front of you. On the left, is a functional MRI of what the average human brain looks like when it is in the process of hoping for something."

He clicks the remote and the screen shows the human brain. It is lit up with many colors. It is beautiful. "Regular MRI, or magnetic resonance imaging, uses a powerful magnetic field and radio waves to give a dimensional view of the organs and tissues of the body. But functional MRI gives us something quite remarkable. It is a view into the blood flow in the brain which captures the magnetic moment of the brain's activity." Luke points to the illuminated image. "You see where there are brilliant pools of color? See how the brain seems to light up? That's where the brain is most engaged. One of the groundbreaking discoveries that Kazu has made is being able to identify what the brain looks like when it is engaged in the act of hoping."

"Are you going to be able to show the functional MRI of my own brain today?" I ask.

"Yes. Now let me warn you not to be alarmed by this image. The activity level is much lower. Here is the scan that we just did of your brain." Luke clicks the remote and what I see on-screen almost makes me cry. I see the walnut-like outline of my brain, but inside it there is almost perfect darkness, except for a flicker of yellow and blue along the edges.

The mall is open but nobody's shopping.

"Wow," I say. "If I felt hopeless *before* coming here today, now I'm *beyond* hopeless. Thanks a lot!"

Luke puts his hand gently on my shoulder. "As you can see, very little of your brain is engaged when you try to hope. That's a problem," he says. "But, Jada, it's nothing to be ashamed about. In fact it confirms there is some scientific basis for your hopelessness. Some of the fundamental connections in your brain chemistry have been severed. During the clinical trials, I saw fMRIs much like yours, worse than yours too. But 86% of the volunteers increased their hope capacity from two times to five times their original capacity."

I keep looking back and forth at the image of what a normal brain looks like and my own. It makes me angry. It isn't fair. But the bigger question is: can The Hope Store really increase hope levels in the hopeless? Is there any cheese down this tunnel or is it just another dead end? Luke slips a color screen print of my brain into a cardboard envelope and hands it to me.

"The last thing we'll do today is the hope installation itself," says Luke. "This part ironically is the shortest part of the whole process. Are you ready?"

"No. But I'm willing."

A blue beam of light encircles my head so that it's blue no matter where I turn. Imagine that I am a very tall lamp and the blue light is a lampshade and you start to get the picture.

The light radiates a cool temperature.

Everything beyond the light shimmers like it's underwater. The walls of the room are wavy. Luke turns my chair around so I'm facing myself in the floor-to-ceiling mirror on the far wall. He opens a small box and throws something into the air over me.

At first I don't know what he's throwing so I duck my head. It appears to be silver confetti. But instead of falling, the confetti hangs there in the air. Then ever so slowly, it begins its descent. I am hypnotized by the silver dots falling in slow-motion around me, and falling in the mirror. I stare at the confetti like a kid watching his first snowfall. Maybe I am that kid.

"Wow, how did you do that?" I ask.

Luke smiles. "Kazu and I have many friends who are inventors. This is called 'slow-falling confetti.' It's made out of a substance that falls slower than any other substance known to man. This confetti falls 37 times slower than the standard stuff. Of course they're trying to find more practical, life-improving applications for it too."

"So this is the hope installation?"

"Yes, this is it. All will become clear tomorrow when you view the hope orientation film."

The slow-falling confetti continues its descent around me. I watch it fall in the mirror. It's really quite pretty. The confetti finally settles to the floor. As each dot of color hits the floor, it makes no sound.

"That's all for today. Over the coming week, I want you to pay attention to any changes in your hope levels, your thought processes, your emotions. Then I'll see you back here next week."

"This has been quite a day. I brought my credit card." I reach into my purse for my card.

"Why don't you settle up with April at the front desk and she can book in your next appointment. We're running our First Timer Special. That gives you 25% off, so it's just $750 for the installation." He points to a sign on the wall which reads: *"Enjoy our Halloween Special. Because life without hope is scary!"*

"That's perfect, Luke."

We walk back toward the lobby. As I approach the front desk, I am stunned by what I see: a large glass bowl filled with purple lotuses blossoms. "Oh my god," I say. I can't take my eyes off the flowers.

"What is it?" asks Luke. "Is something wrong?"

"Where did these come from?" I say. "They weren't here when I came in."

April jumps in. "The investor lady dropped them off for the store opening about an hour ago. She had a funny name."

"Chartreuse?" I say.

"That's it."

Luke just smiles.

"When you were doing my MRI, you asked me to hope for something. This is exactly what I hoped for." I point to the flowers. "Purple lotuses floating in water in a large round bowl. Do you think this is here because I hoped for it?"

Luke is beaming at me, but he isn't gloating as I might have expected. "It's less important what I think and more important what you think. What you *feel*. Does it feel like just a coincidence, or does it feel like something else? I'll see you tomorrow, Jada. Keep your eyes peeled."

I don't know what to say so I say nothing. I take a picture of the lotus blossoms with my smartphone. I pay my bill. When I step out of the store, I look up at the clouds, Clark Street, the pedestrians. The world looks the same. As I walk down the street, every now and then I notice a glimmer out of the corner of my eye. I make a note of it in a small spiral notebook. "Ask Luke about the glimmers."

I leave the store with the knowledge that there may be something new inside of me. I hope my body does not reject the hope as a foreign substance. As I stroll down Clark Street past the Swedish Bakery, past the cute coffeehouses, I keep my eyes peeled for whatever comes my way. I am ready to calibrate even the most microscopic changes in my life. But I am also totally prepared for failure, for disappointment on a grand scale.

"Hope for something, Jada," I whisper to myself. But I am afraid.

"Okay, I wish to have one nice surprise today! It can be big or small, but it's got to be surprising." That is all I wish for. But in a lifetime sadly lacking in surprises, any surprise would be a big deal.

Could I ever be a hopeful person? The mere possibility makes my heart beat faster. And then tears appear unexpectedly. I never cry in public. I barely cry in private. What's going on? The Clark 22 arrives and I climb up the stairs.

The bus driver looks at me with concern. "Are you okay, ma'am?" he asks. And I am aware that I am still crying. I'm embarrassed.

"Oh!" I say. "I'm sorry." I dab at my eyes and sniffle.

"Never apologize for having deep feelings. That's a blessing," he says. "I just want to make sure you're all right is all. This is The Happy Bus. As a rider on this bus, you are entitled, no, you are *required* to have a great ride. Is that okay with you?"

"Excuse me?"

"You heard me." He clicks on his turn signal.

A kind CTA bus driver? Could this be the surprise I was hoping for? Or was it just a coincidence?

"What's your name?" I say. I have never asked a bus driver his name before.

"Walter McGee. Want my badge number too?"

Walter," I say. "Thank you for letting me ride The Happy Bus." And then I lean over and kiss the driver on the cheek. The driver is as shocked as I am.

It's only later after I exit the bus that I realize in all the excitement – I forgot to pay my fare.

LUKE

19. CHECK-IN

Luckily we have a few more customers for our first day. If things keep up, we might have twenty by the end of the day. But I'm dreading our Skype call to Chartreuse.

"Maybe we shouldn't Skype her. How about shooting her a quick email?" Kazu suggests.

"You know she's going to want to talk to us. She'll call us," I say. "We can't pretend to have missed her call. Let's just get it over with. Then we can go have dinner."

I click on the Skype icon on my laptop. Kazu pulls up a chair. We both finger-comb our hair so we're camera-ready. It's likely that the whole investor board will be on-line. I start the Skype call and I hear the familiar futuristic sound. After a few beeps, I see Char's head looming like a balloon on my screen. I can see some of the investors behind her. "Hi everyone!" I say. Kazu waves his hand.

"Congratulations, gentlemen, on The Hope Store's first day of operation," she says in an uncharacteristically upbeat tone. The investors burst into spontaneous applause. "So how did it go?" she asks.

"Well, when Kazu and I arrived at the store, there were dozens of customers lined up at our door! Actually, the line went down Clark Street."

"That's terrific," says one of the investors.

Kazu jumps in. "We asked them if they'd seen any of the CNN coverage of the store. Many had seen it and weren't bothered by the Natural Hoper comments." I nod vigorously.

"How many customers bought hope installations today?" Chartreuse asks.

"Uh, well, let me start by saying we have some good news and some bad news," I say. "The not-so-great news is that the Natural Hopers staged a pretty effective protest outside the store this morning. They handed out very corporate-looking brochures touting natural and inexpensive methods of increasing hope. They also did a good job convincing people that The Hope Store was out to exploit the hopeless and that our treatment was highly experimental and reckless."

"How did that go over?" asks one of the other investors.'

"Unfortunately it went over much better than we would have thought," Kazu says.

"Bottom line," I say, "nineteen clients paid for hope installations today. At $750 per, that comes to $14,250 total. It's not great but it's a start."

Chartreuse looks like a balloon on the verge of exploding. "Didn't I tell you, Luke, that we had to do damage control. What part of that did you not understand?"

"Chartreuse, Kazu and I think this is a temporary setback. We have had enough phone calls and emails to book us solid for the rest of the week. Which brings me to the great news."

"And what would that be?" she asks.

"Well, nothing is definite," I say, "but I got a phone call today from *Psychology Tomorrow*. They're considering running a piece on The Hope Store. But they want to wait and see what kind of results we get first."

"Well, let's give them some Super-Responder to write about! Do you have any promising candidates?"

I think for a moment. "There is one that comes to mind. Jada Upshaw has been chronically hope-deprived most of her life. If she has a good response, she could be very inspiring."

"I like that," Chartreuse says. "Keep us in the loop, fellas." She ends the Skype call with the usual Skype bleep.

JADA

20. WEEK OF WONDERS

I am monitoring myself these weeks for any changes in perception, in behavior. But now I just have to clean my neglected house. Generally, I start out with good intentions and wind up playing solitaire on the computer.

But today I pick up a mop and fill a bucket with soap and water. I attack the kitchen floor with an energy that startles me. And that growing pile of dirty dishes that has towered in the sink? Those dishes are now clean and drying in the rack. I even throw in a few loads of laundry while I'm at it. All day I watch my hands move like propellers. It is as if they are not my own. My legs too are in on the conspiracy, taking me on errands to places I've never been. When I'm done, I return home, ease back in the recliner and drink a frosty glass of Diet Dr. Pepper. It hits the spot. The bubbles tickle my nose. For weeks I haven't been able to eat a proper meal at the kitchen table as it's covered with a jigsaw puzzle depicting a city of the future. The puzzle spills over with laser beams and translucent buildings and hovercrafts.

I wanted to take a picture of the future before I dismantled it.

But who has time for such frivolity when you're on a mission? I put the puzzle pieces back into the box and reclaim the kitchen table.

After my house cleaning, I go over to crash at Otis' place. I give him the latest scoop. "So The Hope Store party was very cool. I wish you came along," I say. "CNN was there. Oh, but when we were leaving the party, we saw someone had vandalized the store sign."

"What'd they do to it?"

"Well, the store sign is made out of these powder-blue neon letters that spell THE HOPE STORE. Someone covered the "O" with a "Y" so it read THE HYPE STORE!"

"How rude," says Otis.

He is watching some football on TV. But when there is a break in the action, he continues. "So how did you get into the party without an invite?"

"I batted my lashes and pretended to be a dumb blond. Which is a stretch for me, let me tell ya. But it worked like a charm." He laughs. "I was really determined to get some hope juice, Otis. So I got my installation yesterday."

He rubs his temples. "Really? Are you feeling anything?"

"I really don't," I say. "If the whole thing turns out to be scammy as I think it might be, there's a friend who wants to write up my experience for the papers."

"So..." he says.

"What?"

"So how do you get the hope juice inside your brain?"

"Well, if you'd come to the party, you'd be an expert like me by now."

"Are you feeling more hopeful today than you felt yesterday?"

"It's too soon to say," I tell him. "I'll keep you posted."

The next night, Otis crashes at my place. I have to feed Shadow and keep her company or she'll start acting weird. We are getting ready for bed when I see the glimmer again. What *is* that? Otis climbs into bed. He has such a nice body, so lean and wiry. And his manner is so gentle. Why do I always take him for granted? Truth is we haven't had sex in years. Usually, this is where I set the alarm and we turn away from each other and fall asleep. But tonight is different. Tonight is spicy. I put my hand gently on Otis' strong shoulder. I spoon my body against Otis' back side. I grip his muscular chest with one hand and bite his ear lobe. And we proceed to have the most ferocious sex we've had in years.

Afterward, we just lie back and catch our breaths. "Wow," is all he can say. "You don't know how long I've waited for you to make love to me like that."

"I know, right?" I say. "I don't know where that came from."

"Don't apologize," says Otis.

Suddenly I turn to him and say, "Otis, do you want to have a baby?"

And it really is a dumb question as Otis has always wanted to have kids while I have not.

He blinks. Then he says, "Who are you?" He carefully examines the front and back of my hands. "Are you some kind of alien? What have you done with my girlfriend?"

And in that moment, the temperature in the room changes. The sparks of sexual passion mutate into suspicion. I have become the Girlfriend from the Other Planet. I'm pretty sure I'm not an alien. But I don't quite feel like myself either. And what was so great about the Old Jada anyway?

Sheila's home is decorated with cornucopia galore and gourds of all shapes and colors. Construction paper turkeys haunt the living room windows. One cannot enter this house without remembering that Thanksgiving is just around the corner. Sheila has some of her special sweet potato pie baking in the oven. All I have to do is pull it out of the oven. Once again I am inspired to tell my niece and nephew something true, something useful.

Now that I have had my hope installation, I'm curious what my message will be. Actually, I'm nervous what my message will be.

"Kids, I'm no fortune teller. Will your life stories have a happy ending? I couldn't tell you. I hope so. But that's pretty much up to you. Hope is the engine to get you where you want to go, but you're still driving the car. You're still the one behind the steering wheel, filling up the tank, listening to the GPS. But if you have hope, you're halfway home. Does that make sense?"

Willis looks unconvinced. "Mom said that you were born without hope. How did that happen?"

"That's a good question, Willis. I'm not really sure," I say. "But since I got my hope installation…" And now I'm at a loss for words. I'm getting choked up.

"Are you okay, Auntie," says Angie. "Do you need some Kleenex?"

"I'm fine. Since I got my new hope, my whole life feels new." I call up and order pizza and salads for the three of us. The food will arrive soon.

"At The Hope Store, there are these two cool guys named Kazu and Luke," I say. "They're partners. They love each other, just like your mom and dad Maybe you'll meet them one day. Why don't you watch TV till the food comes?"

When the doorbell rings, everyone is excited.

I lift the pizza slices onto paper plates, pour soda for the three of us.

"Did you know that some people are born with natural talents and some are born without? When Kazu and Luke aren't at the store, they're in the laboratory trying to figure out how to trick the brain into doing more than if can now."

"I know how to make people smile, Aunt Jada," says the little one. "Is that a talent?"

"That is a very special talent."

It's been a week since my installation and tonight I'm going to The Hope Store to debrief. As I approach the store it's as if I'm seeing it for the first time. How did I not notice the dazzling beacon of light over the store's entrance, winking at passersby? The light is so bright it could guide ships to safety.

The inside of the store strikes me as a not-unpleasing cross between a health spa and a movie theatre multiplex, with blue votive candles illuminating the perimeter of the main floor. Along the walls are screening rooms with little movies playing on monitors, are they scenes from their lives? The customer and facilitator speak gently to each other. Are they praying or finalizing sales transactions?

As I stroll through the corridor, I look into the large glass windows of activity rooms. In one room, a South Asian woman stands in front of a screen revealing hand-held footage from an earthquake. Buildings collapse in slow motion, citizens run for their lives. The woman holds a silver locket in her hand and weeps. In another room, there is a somber Caucasian family. On-screen I see the blueprint of a house, with pictures of the mother, father, and child each confined to separate rooms, each one is typing on a computer. In another room, I see a teenage boy doing some kind of interpretive dance in front of images of Keith Haring cartoon images, though the dance's meaning is lost on me.

"These are images of hope and hopelessness," says a young woman's voice behind me. "They come from the minds of our customers." It is April, the woman from the front desk. Her voice is calm and soothing, not giddy as I remember from the soft opening. "Customers are encouraged to express their lives through movement and memory, or to channel their inner demons onto a small movie screen."

Jada smiles. "Luke and I haven't gotten to the activity rooms yet."

"The activity rooms are extra," April explains. "They're supplemental to the treatment." It strikes me that though there is a reverential tone at the store, though religion has never been brought into the mix. That suits me. Personally, I like a clean separation between church and psyche.

A tall man with searching eyes stands at a kiosk and nods at me. He wears a simple black dress shirt. But when he turns around, I see written on his back in shiny silver letters are the words: "Begin to hope." I notice these shirts are also for sale on a clothes rack. There are hope accessories everywhere I turn. And why shouldn't there be? Another shirt says: "Hope is the engine that moves you forward." I decide to buy one of each: for Otis and me.

Finally, it's time. I walk into Luke's office. "Greetings, stranger," says Luke. "You look radiant."

"Hey, Luke."

"So please tell me how have things been going? Did you notice anything new?"

"I don't know where to start."

"Then just start anywhere," he says.

And I begin to tell him about my weeks of wonder. "My sister Sheila and I go shopping together at Target. Have you ever been in a Target store, Luke? You know how their red circle logo is everywhere and there are bright red walls next to the escalator which takes you down to the underground parking lot?"

"Right."

"When I ride that escalator to the garage, I always feel like I'm descending into purgatory and that the happy giant faces on the wall are mocking me. But when I went to Target last week, I didn't feel that way," I say.

"How did you feel?"

"I felt the logo was just a logo. The bright red walls reminded me of cherry lipstick, not hell. I actually enjoyed shopping at Target. That's never happened before."

"When a person accumulates more dopamine, they naturally feel more positive," Luke explains. "There can be global benefits that go beyond feeling hopeful. You can also feel more open, more awake even. Some people notice their memory improves, or food tastes better. Hope level increases can have both local and global effects."

"Here's another thing," I say. "I always liked doing art projects when I was younger, but after a certain age, I stopped. Last week, I found myself making a diorama. I took an old shoe box and cut out figures to create a scene, a little slice of life. I made one for you." I reach into my shopping bag and pull out a box and place it on Luke's desk. It is a diorama of The Hope Store. Blue tinfoil creates the neon sign bearing the store's name. Through the window, one can see a tiny waterfall behind the tiny reception desk. And standing out front of the store are little paper cut-outs of Luke and Kazu."

"It's wonderful, Jada. Very creative," he says.

"Do you really like it?"

"No, I don't really like it. I love it."

I'm thrilled. "Oh, I started to look for work again. Even though the job market is still crummy, I just have a good feeling that there might be a great job waiting for me with my name on it. It's not logical really."

"Hope doesn't have to be logical to help you," Luke says.

I don't tell him about my housekeeping adventures or that I asked Otis if he wanted to start

125

a family. There's too much to tell and a girl has to keep some secrets to herself.

People who've survived their suicide attempts tell their loved ones that it wasn't so much that they wanted to die. It was that they wanted to end the pain of being alive. There is a difference. It's a difference lost on most.

-- What the Living Can Learn from the Suicidal
   Victoria Chase

JADA

21. COMPLEX

Blair Matters and I are having drinks at Reservoir. It is a chatty Thursday crowd that seems to be chomping at the bit for Friday. We are both drinking today's special: pear martinis. "Blair, I'm so glad you could meet. Today was a very juicy day at The Hope Store. I hope you can use some of what I share with you for your story."

"I'm all ears, Jada." He stirs his martini with his finger. "All fingers too." He licks a few digits.

"Well," I begin, "I have to say this story is much more...uh, uh...what do you call it?"

"Give me a hint. Sounds like?"

"Uh, you know, I mean it's not a simple story..."

"Complex? This story is much more complex than you expected?"

"Exactly! Thank you."

Several pear martinis later, I have told Blair all about the nasty protesters from the Natural Hopers, recounted how I was subjected to a brain scan and all sorts of new age nonsense, and finally got my hope installation. I give him both the protesters' pamphlet and The Hope Store's pamphlet and Blair plans to draft a story tonight.

And then I mention the lotus blossoms. How I don't know quite what to make of them.

"Hold the phone," he says. "Are you telling me you think this hope installation somehow magically conjured up these flowers because you hoped for them?

"Of course not," I say. "That would be crazy, right?"

Blair just shakes his head. "Oh shit. You've gone and drunk the Kool-Aid, haven't you?"

"I'm sure the flowers were just a weird coincidence. I'm going to see how things progress -- or fail to progress -- over the next few weeks," I say. "

"Hold the phone. Are you telling me you're actually feeling more *hopeful* since your trip to The Hope Store?"

"Well, uh, am I feeling more hopeful," I say.

Blair is thoroughly disgusted. "Then, Houston, we have a problem. Because we no longer have an exposé in progress. We have a puff piece. And Blair Matters may do a lot of bullshit to make a buck, but he doesn't do puff pieces."

"Like I was saying, Blair, the story has turned out to be more complex than I expected."

He tosses some bills on the table. "Thanks for being such a loyal partner, Jada. Thanks for helping restart my career. Thanks for nothing," he says. "I hope your hope installation has horrible side effects. And if there's any way I can make you sorry for this -- I will."

Blair Matters walks out the door and never looks back.

I have Otis on my cell's speakerphone, as I check email on my laptop. He's eager to know how my treatment is going. My cat Shadow jumps up onto my desk and nudges her head against my hand. I pet her for a while, scratching under her neck.

"So what are you feeling exactly? Be specific."

"There was this glimmer...out of the corner of my eye," I say. "Do you know what I mean?"

"I have no idea what you're talking about."

"And there was other stuff too," I say thinking about the lotus flowers that I seemed to manifest at the store. On my huge flat screen TV, I notice there is a commercial for The Hope Store. It's alluring and mysterious...confetti falling in slow motion.

"You're a tease, you know that?" Otis says.

"Otis, sweetie, I wish I could tell you more but I haven't really, what do you call it, *processed* it all. I'll keep you in the loop."

JADA

22. AT THE MOVIES

When I return to the store the next day, there are new flowers at the front desk. White tulips this time. I lean over and inhale their delicate scent. Kazu comes out to say hi.

"How is the treatment going? Is Luke behaving himself?" Kazu asks.

"Luke is amazing. I'm so happy you two have found each other."

"We have to catch up over a meal soon," Kazu says. "I'm sure a lot has happened for you in the past ten years."

"Oh, don't be so sure. Really, my life is pretty dull compared to yours."

"I'll call you to arrange dinner," he says.

And soon I am in Luke's office. "Today I'm going to show you a short film that should help fill in some blanks," says Luke. "We were dying to have it ready for the press opening, but the technology gods had other ideas. It's mainly important for a Hope Orientation Session with new clients."

"I love movies." He guides me to sit down on a small wooden bench. Then he pushes the remote and a movie screen rises up from out of the floor! The screen is curved like a parenthesis to surround me. It's about ten feet across and five feet high.

"Just relax and enjoy the show." Luke uses the remote to turn off the lights in his office.

My eyes are riveted to the screen. Emblazoned on the screen are the words: "The Biology of Hope." The movie starts. A full-size image of Luke Nagano walks onscreen. It startles me and I gasp. There Luke is onscreen, big as life.

"Hi, welcome to The Hope Store. I hope I didn't startle you. I know you have many questions and we'll try to answer the main ones with this little movie. My name is Luke Nagano and this is Kazu Mori."

Luke looks off-screen but no one comes.

"Uh, I said...and this is Kazu Mori!"

Kazu now walks in from the opposite side of the curved screen. He waves a bit sheepishly into the camera.

"Hi, everybody. I'm a bit camera-shy so... So let's get started with Question 1, shall we?"

Onscreen, in a very large font, are the words: "Question 1: WHAT IS HOPE?" Animated image of a crowd bustling in a busy downtown. One cartoon man stops at a window display of a car dealership to admire a gleaming new car. Luke's onscreen self speaks.

"So what, you may well ask, is hope really? We turn to psychiatrist Shana Rosenstein, consultant for the project."

Ms. Rosenstein is seated apparently in her psychiatrist's office, a long paisley couch is in the background.

"Of course many people define hope as getting everything they've ever dreamt of! That's more wishful thinking than anything else. Or some say hope is something that a religion or philosophy gives you to make a person strong. And certainly hope can come from many different sources. But the dictionary definition is actually much more simple and pure. And we scientists like simple."

The dictionary definition of "hope" flashes onto the screen:

1. the feeling that the thing you most want, you can have.

2. the confidence that a desired goal can be achieved.

3. optimism, confidence in a future outcome.

There is a sunny shot of Luke standing in front of The Hope Store. He speaks. *"In fact, it has been said that hope is the engine of everything we do. Have you ever tried to drive a car without an engine? It's hard."*

Cut to the cartoon man in his cartoon car. He is pumping the gas pedal but nothing is happening. The man frowns. Then a thought bubble above his head reveals a picture of him in that gleaming new car and he smiles. The man walks on his merry way.

Onscreen are the words: "Question 2: WHAT IS THE BIOLOGY OF HOPE?" This footage is very modern and high tech. There are rows and rows of test tubes in racks filled with colorful solutions. Spinning centrifuges.

Now there is a shot of Luke in The Hope Store waiting area, reading a magazine. He puts down the magazine and speaks to us.

"What role does our body play in creating hope? For that, we turn to bio-tech scientist Kazu Mori, co-creator with me of The Hope Store."

Screen goes to black. The first image we make out looks like an asteroid spinning through space. But it is actually a human brain. It slowly spins to a stop.

"So let's start at the beginning, with the human brain. Simply put, within the brain there are neurotransmitters whose job is to help parts of the brain talk to each other."

There is a cartoon image of a little stick figure man talking on the phone to a stick figure woman. They are depicted as residing within the brain.

"Dopamine is the neurotransmitter that, when released, inspires hope in us. We've known this since the 1970s. But what we've been trying to figure out is how to create more of it. Interesting footnote: because dopamine involves the way we view the future, it has been dubbed by

some as 'the chemical of anticipation.' If that ain't poetry, I don't know what is."

Close-up on stick lady laughing on phone.

"So we've got the neurotransmitters chatting away and all is groovy. But for some reason or another, the connection breaks up. The reception's bad. Who knows? And in hopeless people, those neurotransmitters are just plain broken. Messages never reach their destinations."

The telephone line snaps in two. Question marks float over both stick figure heads.

"So when the need for hope arises -- the request for dopamine never reaches its destination. And so the hope order goes unfilled. The Hope Store has found a way to magnetically stimulate the part of the brain which releases dopamine, tricking the brain into creating surplus amounts of the stuff. This was a major breakthrough, essentially learning how to trick the brain to heal itself. Powerful magnetic waves surround the client in the Installation Suite. And a metallic slow-falling confetti acts as a catalyst when released over the subject's head."

In a cartoon image, magnetic fields are represented by lightning bolts hovering over the brain. And then...the slow descent of silver confetti around the client.

Onscreen are the words: "Question 3: WHAT CAN YOU EXPECT TO EXPERIENCE AFTER YOUR HOPE INSTALLATION?" Music segues underneath, mystical without being maudlin.

135

Shana Rosenstein peers into a microscope. She looks up. *"You can expect that you'll start a whole new chapter in your life."*

The cartoon man who dreams of buying a new car is now in the driver's seat. *"You can expect that you'll never again drive an engineless car,"* he says. The man puts on some sunglasses and drives out of the frame.

Kazu stands in front of a chalkboard filled with chemical symbols and formulas. *"Hope is the force underlying much of human endeavor. It is inextricably bound up with the future. And it will be inextricably bound up with your future too."* I find myself getting emotional.

The onscreen Luke stands in front of the dramatic waterfall at the center of the store. *"At The Hope Store, we don't just instill hope. We <u>install it</u>."*

He snaps his fingers and looks up expectantly. Beautiful confetti of all colors falls in super slow-motion from above. He and Kazu pick up glasses of champagne and make a toasting gesture toward the camera. *"Cheers!"* As the image of the two men slows to a freeze frame, the logo of The Hope Store and slogan appear at the bottom of the screen which fades to a blind white.

I stand up and clap, even though it's just a movie. "I want some more hope! You made me cry, darn you." But when I step outside the parenthesis, I don't see Luke anywhere. "Luke?"

I wander out into the hallway and see the stairwell door open. So I start climbing the stairs because I see a light above and feel the cold outside air. When I get to the third floor, I see the roof door is open. I step out. Luke is there taking in the skyline.

"I didn't know where you'd gone," I say.

"The air is different up here. It's cleaner. I was watching the movie and suddenly I felt…I don't know, anxious. It was hard to catch my breath. So I came up here where it's peaceful. Maybe it was a panic attack. I'm sorry I left you –"

"Not a problem," I say. "The movie was terrific. Are you feeling better now?"

"We should get back. Before they send a search party." He smiles.

"But you're feeling better, right, with the fresh air?" I say.

"You really should see the view from this roof at night. It'll change your life, Jada." I sense he really loves it up here. We slowly make our way down the three flights of stairs in silence. I don't ask him again if he's okay. And he doesn't tell me.

LUKE

23. A DIMMING

There was a moment.
In my office.
With Jada.
When I felt a shadow fall across me.

In that moment I was terrified that I was having a relapse. That my hopefulness had been stolen away. In that irrational moment, The Hope Store had never been invented. Other subjects in the clinical trials sometimes reported similar feelings. If the first sign of new hope entering the subject is the *glimmer* out of the corner of one's eye, then the opposite of a glimmer surely is a kind of *dimming*. Both sensations are premonitions of a change in brain chemistry. One subject reported he had "a dimming" in the middle of a birthday party. Another had a dimming during sexual intercourse. Yet another had a dimming while giving a speech. Sometimes the dimming is a sign that the individual needs another installation. But sometimes this is a symptom of a bigger problem.

When I get back to my office, I see a printout of the Tribune follow-up story on my desk along with a scribbled post-it from April saying, "Hell's bells! Do you know anything about this *Psychology Tomorrow* article?" I read on with great interest.

From the Culture Beat blog of the Chicago Tribune
"Keeping Hope Alive & Kicking" by Madeline Worth

Last month, I mentioned a new venture in town called The Hope Store, a store that makes the bold claim they can install hope into the hopeless. Would it turn out to be the hottest thing since Apple turned its competitors into applesauce, or would it be a lemon? Their first month's gross sales have been lackluster, thanks in large part to strategic protests staged by the Natural Hopers, as well as push-back from an array of talking heads, bloggers, and jealous scientists.

But don't give up hope on The Hope Store just yet. The store has been steadily building a client base of repeat customers and Yelp reviews have been overwhelmingly positive. Rumor has it Psychology Tomorrow is considering doing a write-up on the store. If that comes to pass, watch for a major sales bump at The Hope Store! Come to think of it, a hope installation would make an amazing holiday gift for the friend who has almost everything.

This has got to be one of the most thrilling bad reviews I've ever read. I'll have to see if anyone can confirm the PT rumor. If it's a false rumor, that'll be a shame. But if it's true, this could be the big break we've been hoping for.

I'm dying to stroll over to Kazu's office and see what he might know. That's when I discover that Kazu knows all about the magazine coverage. Apparently, they wanted to talk to the science guy rather than the marketing guy. Kazu wanted to keep it under wraps so that it would be a surprise when the issue came out. The magazine is especially interested in profiling Jada. We agree that Kazu can talk to her about it when they have their reunion dinner.

✦

In my sessions with Jada, it's impossible not to notice her hope levels rising like waves in an ocean. The world that spins beneath her feet is the same world but her view of it is completely different. She finds herself talking Otis' ear off late at night in bed. All the things she wants to be when she grows up: a toy designer, a talk show host, a neurosurgeon, a cop. She finds herself wanting things she's never wanted before. "Maybe we could start a family, Otis." "Maybe we could take that trip to India we used to talk about." And suddenly *maybe* starts to sound like *might be.*

Here is one way to understand Jada's transformation. It's as if all her life, she has pictured herself standing in a torrential rainstorm under a broken-down umbrella. But what if that storm was imagined, a hallucination? What if in fact it has been bright and sunny all along? Having an enhanced level of hope allows her to see that, allows her to throw that broken-down umbrella into the trash where it belongs. If there are Natural Hopers in the world, Jada would surely be part of that other breed: the *Enhanced Hopers.*

JADA

24. HOPERS IN TRANSITION

We are in the back room at Two-Hearted Queen, a charming café owned by a lesbian couple. The staff has allowed us to push two long rectangular tables together to form a huge square one. Around the table, I see faces -- some of them familiar from The Hope Store, most of them not.

This is the first assembly of a Meetup group called "Enhanced Hopers." Even though it's new, the Meetup home page shows that 1,546 people have already joined. The group organizer Terrance has done some impressive polling of the membership and explained in his welcoming email that of the 1,546 members, 178 have actually had hope installations. And who are the other 1,368? They are the hope-curious, the fence-sitters. In short, they are the lurkers.

"Thanks to everyone for coming here to the first meeting of Enhanced Hopers. My name is Terrance and I'm the organizer," says the smartly dressed black man. He wears sky-blue suspenders over a chocolate brown dress shirt. "Though there are about 25 of us here today, there was quite a waiting list. To be honest, the membership is growing so fast -- this may also be our *last* meeting."

Everyone looks surprised, some laugh nervously.

I half-raise my hand. "Hi, my name is Jada. I'm just curious why it would be our last meeting if the group is growing so fast."

"Excellent question," he says. "The reason is purely a logistical one. It was hard finding a space that could accommodate a group this size. We might do better to gather together online in the future via chat room, bulletin board or Skype."

I nod and sip my latte.

"Why don't we go around and have everyone say their name. Then tell us if you've had a hope installation and where you are on a scale from 1 to 5, with 5 indicating a great response."

A tall, handsome Latino man clears his throat. "I'll start. My name is Madrid and if you asked me last week, I'd have said I was a 4, maybe a 4.2, but today I'm a solid 5. This week has been amazing. I'm starting my dream job on Thursday!"

"Thanks for sharing the good news, Madrid." Terrance looks to the next woman around the table.

"My name is Lucinda and I guess I'm one of the lurkers," she says shyly. "I'm saving up for an installation. But even with the discount, the price is $750 and...well, let's just say I don't have that kind of money sitting around in a cookie jar at home."

The group laughs.

A woman with retro eyeglasses and an equally retro paisley dress is next. "The past few weeks have been amazing. Definitely a 5. Final answer. My kids even notice the difference. I'm not moping around the house like I usually do. I'm starting new projects, and finishing them too. I'm multi-tasking like a madwoman."

A middle-aged man waves to the group. "Hi, everyone. My name is Luther. To be honest I'd have to give myself a 3, but then I'm pretty new. I'm glad you all started this support group. I kinda feel like I've found my tribe."

And so it goes.

Everyone has a story to tell, many of them are transformative. That is, until Mimi speaks.

"Wow, I guess I'm in the minority here. I'm Mimi and I have to say I'm a zero today. I'm so disappointed with The Hope Store I could spit. They say I'm a Low Responder but I'd say I'm a No Responder. I'm dying to know why you guys are so jazzed and why my hope tank is so damn empty. I really want to know."

The organizer nods. "Thanks, Mimi. Maybe we can talk about that later."

"I mean, I'm just being honest," she says. "You don't want me to lie, do you? Can I help it if I haven't drunk the Kool-Aid like some folks around this table."

Terrance tries to remain composed. "I don't think anyone's drunk any Kool-Aid, Mimi. I think people just have different experiences and we need to honor those experiences. Don't you agree?"

"I just know what I know. Maybe it wasn't such a hot idea me coming to this group."

"Why's that?" asks Madrid.

"Because I told Kazu and Luke that I demand a full refund and if I don't get one -- I just might sue them." A silence falls over the conversation.

I look at Terrance. He tries to remain unruffled. "Why don't we finish with the introductions. Then we'll see what the group wants to talk about. How's that?" he asks, but I know he's not asking anyone. He's telling them.

JADA

25. YOU ARE HERE

Kazu and I are finally having our long-awaited catch-up dinner at Leona's. I won't pretend that I have done wonderful things in the past ten years since I took that class with him. I'm tired of pretending. The hope installation is not just giving more hope. I feel an increase in my courage too. How are hope and courage related? Which leads to the other?

I find myself in a bit of a pickle. Having laid the trap to help expose the store as a scam – I am in the unlikely position of being cured. My hope levels have increased in ways big and small. And the fMRI at the end of a month's time will confirm what my simple experiences cannot: that the change is not just in my imagination but in my body as well.

Blair Matters accuses me of having drunk the Kool-Aid. But how else could I become a true guinea pig? It's not my fault the Kool-Aid was so tasty. He is furious at me for wasting his time and I can understand that. I did tell him I'd still give him an exclusive: he could write up my adventures at The

Hope Store. The only thing is, it would just have a very different ending. His passion is consumer advocacy. He said it was becoming abundantly clear that there was no longer a project we could collaborate upon.

Kazu strolls into Leona's and I wave him over to our booth. Again, we hug since we are old friends. Never mind that I had a crush on the guy ten years ago and that he has gotten more dashing with age. He's got a partner after all.

"Finally," he says, and we both know what that means. It's taken a while for us to have our catch-up-on-old-times dinner.

"Well, it's been a crazy time for you with the store opening," I say.

"And, Jada, I know Luke has probably said something but I want to personally say how much it meant to me that first day when the Natural Hopers made such a ruckus —"

"Kazu," I start, not wanting to be eulogized again. "It was nothing. Believe me."

"—they succeeded in scaring our customers away that day. But you stayed!"

"Kazu, listen to me. All those noble reasons you and Luke keep attributing to me — those aren't the reasons I stayed." I have his attention at last.

"Really. Then why? Why did you stay?"

I take a deep sip of my Diet Dr. Pepper, wishing I was drinking something so much harder, much more distilled or fermented. "Please don't be hurt by what I'm about to say, Kazu."

"Hurt? I don't think you could hurt me if you wanted to."

I look at my old friend and choose my words carefully. "The reason I came to The Hope Store was...I wanted to prove that the hope installation *wouldn't* work."

Kazu smiles. He takes a moment to digest my statement. "Jada, it's the most natural thing in the world to be skeptical."

"You see, being hope-deprived my whole life, I've been disappointed by so many quacks offering magic cures for my suffering. When I first heard about the store, it made me angry. I wanted to show people, to warn them not to be made fools of. I didn't know at the time you were involved."

"Jada." I see his face get more serious as it dawns on him what I'm saying.

I continue to make my full confession. "I talked to a journalist about writing about my trials and tribulations at The Hope Store. He was *very* interested. I was so sure...that the store was just selling more snake oil, more hope in a jar. I didn't expect..."

"What? What didn't you expect?" Kazu asks.

"...I didn't expect the hope installation to work! I didn't see that coming."

There is a long pause. It's not my place to fill it. The waiter comes and Kazu and I place our dinner orders. We sip our drinks. I wonder if he will ever speak to me again, if this dinner will take place from hereon in utter silence.

"So…this journalist…" he starts.

"Oh, as soon as I started to have a great response to the installation, he bailed. That story is not going to happen."

"I see," he says. "That story could have hurt us."

"I didn't want to hurt anyone. I just wanted to protect people like me." I eat a stale breadstick.

"You said at the time, you didn't know I was involved?"

"That's right."

"And once you knew I was involved, that my life partner was involved…you still pursued the exposé?"

I know where Kazu is going with this so I must choose my words carefully. "It was a very hard decision to make," I say. "I don't know if you can understand. Maybe if I tell you how I spent the last, lost decade of my life… It wasn't *personal*, Kazu. "

"When you try to tear down someone's dream…that's personal, Jada. Goddammit. I don't know who you are anymore, Jada. Or who you ever were. I can't even sit with you right now."

" I've never seen him so angry, so hurt. What have I done? He gets up and paces restlessly. Then he makes a beeline to the men's room.

"I fucked up," I say to an empty table. "I'm a bad person," I mention to my glass of iced tea. Its lemon wedge winks at me. "I don't feel well at all," I confess to anyone in the restaurant who will listen.

I look up and there is the waiter standing before me with an offering in his hand. "Calamari?" he says and I don't think I've ever been less hungry in my life. This is how friendships break apart. Out of the corner of my eye, I see Kazu making his way back to our table. I study his body language, his expression. Neutral.

"I'm so sorry. I totally fucked up. How can I make this right again, Kazu?"

He looks deep into my eyes and I'm afraid what he can see. "I was standing in the men's room taking a leak. I was really mad at you, but I knew this was my karma. I couldn't blame you though I wanted to. This was my chance to learn something or to learn nothing."

"Did you learn something?"

"Not yet. Just that I'm hungry," he says.

"You guys really have something amazing that the world needs," I say. "I did consider not telling you...about my original agenda. But I see you and Luke as more than just...store owners. I see you as friends. But of course...I don't know, uh, well, you know..."

"What?" he asks.

"I don't know how you see me. How you see me *now*."

Kazu looks at me.

Then he stands up. I'm terrified he's walking out in the middle of dinner. "Let's try this again." Kazu stands up, turns around, and looks surprised. "Jada, so good to see you!"

"You too, Kazu," I reply.

"I just wanted you to know, Jada, and I really hope this doesn't hurt your feelings but...I just wanted to tell you a personal secret. *About me.* You see, I don't hug my customers. I only hug my friends."

And in this moment, Kazu seems further away from me than he's ever been before. He looks at me with a blank face which tells me nothing. Then Kazu embraces me, and I feel like I can breathe again.

"Shall we eat? I'm starving," he says.

Sometimes a moment comes up that you have to smooth over with your hand. Kazu has done that. Somehow he has made all the calculations in his head at lightning speed. He has determined that our friendship is bigger than this, this...stumble. He is a better person than I will ever be, and for that, I am grateful grateful grateful.

"I wanted to have dinner with you to catch up, but there's another reason," Kazu says.

"Really? By all means catch me up," I say.

"I have the printout of your latest fMRI. This shows your brain activity and engagement a month after your installation. I didn't want to show it to you till I could confirm its validity."

"Ok, now I'm dying to see it."

He puts two color printouts side by side. The first one is a darkened walnut of a brain with just a trickle of light on one side. But the new one looks like the Fourth of July.

"When you first came to the store, your dopamine level was at 12%. Now? It's at 72%"

I'm speechless. A few tears roll down my face. "Oh my god. Is that all me?

"That is all you, Jada. You are not just a Good Responder. We call people like you...a Super Responder."

I let out a laugh.

"Oh and something else," he says. "There has been some media interest in you."

"In me?"

Of all our clients in our first month of operation, many have had terrific results. But yours has been extraordinary. *Psychology Tomorrow* is interested in doing a profile of you. Actually, it would be the cover story for their next issue. People can use an extra dose of hope during the holidays."

I feel like I'm dreaming. Things like this do not happen to Jada Upshaw.

"They should interview you and Luke. You're the ones who discovered everything."

"They'll talk to us too. So are you interested, Jada? It could mean a lot for The Hope Store."

"But I'm kind of a private person. At least, I've always been a private person before. I don't know what I am now."

"Just say the word, and I'll have them give you a call to set things up. They're very excited to talk to you!"

"Can I think about it? Maybe talk to Otis about it?"

"Sure. But they'd need an answer tomorrow because —"

I try to picture what this would look like: being interviewed by a national magazine, seeing my face on the cover of *Psychology Tomorrow* at Barnes & Noble. Will I be a stuttering fool, or will I knock it out of the park? "Well then...yes. My answer is yes. Final answer."

"Are you sure? I don't want you to feel pressured."

"They say opportunity knocks only once. Isn't that what they say, Kazu?" I take a long, deep sip of my Diet Dr. Pepper.

LUKE

26. DOGHOUSE

When we get home, Kazu and I snack on hummus and pita bread as we watch the news. It took courage for Jada to share her big secret with me. It makes me wonder if I should tell Kazu about the secrets I have been keeping from him.

A segment comes on about the Natural Hopers, once again railing about the dangers of our store. Natural Hoper-in-chief Robert Chang preaches on. "I'm sure The Hope Store creators are decent enough folks. But what they're selling is not only dangerous, it's addictive. Once you get treated, they insist you return for an annual booster installation. At $1,000 a pop, The Hope Store is a gold mine."

"With all due respect, Mr. Chang, do you have any proof that the installations are dangerous?" says Andrew Konstant.

"Do you have any proof they're not? Three years is hardly enough study time for a procedure as potentially significant and clearly invasive as this one."

I flick the remote, turning down the sound. It makes me too angry to listen to him rant. Maybe a town hall meeting wouldn't be such a bad idea. A chance for us to meet our detractors face to face.

"I guess it's pretty obvious who messed with our sign at the press opening," says Kazu.

"Who?" I say.

"Robert Chang would be a good guess. Who else could it be?"

"Yeah, he's a likely suspect."

I have never been great at keeping secrets. I inherited my openness, my big mouth, from my mother. And now this seems like the perfect moment. A new year will soon be upon us. It's time to start with a clean slate.

"I think he's the *only* suspect," insists Kazu. "Can you think of anyone else who has the motive, the balls?"

"Yeah, I can actually," I say.

"Who?" Kazu asks. He faces me as the voice of the Natural Hoper drones in the background.

"Mmm…"

"Who?" he asks.

"Me?"

"Is there something you want to tell me, Luke?" Kazu asks. I don't like the look on his face. There is an anger beneath his smile that I've never seen before. It startles me.

"Now before either of us blows our cools, let me just reiterate that I handle all things related to marketing of the store, and you handle all things related to the science –"

Kazu cuts me off. "Are you saying that you were the one that messed up our sign?"

"Now because you are a man of science, I don't expect you will understand the mysterious ways of marketing." I don't know if he's getting my gentle joke here. Talking down to him about marketing as he talked down to me about science.

For a moment, Kazu rubs his large Japanese hand over his face. "Why would you do that? And why would you not tell me you were going to do that? That's all I want to hear you say."

"In marketing," I say, "we learn that even bad press is good press for a new business. Because it gets people talking, it gets your name out there. I think it made our debut even more...*newsworthy*. I wanted to tell you but I thought you would say no." I watch Kazu's face to see how he's reacting. A big grin spreads across his face.

"That really works, getting bad press?" he says.

"Sometimes it backfires, but in our case I think it helped."

"You funny Americans," Kazu says. "No matter how long I live here, I don't think I'll ever be as American as you. I'm not sure I'd want to be."

"Really. So you're kind of okay with this, you're not --"

"I wish you'd told me about it in the beginning. I wish you'd trusted that I'd have an open mind."

"I'm really sorry, Kazu."

He bursts out laughing. "I just wanted to hear you apologize. That is one of the dumbest marketing schemes I've heard."

"But it worked."

"Did it? How do you know how many customers stayed home because of that stunt?"

"Well…"

"That's a deep subject, that *well* of yours. Be careful you don't fall into it. Please don't ever pull a stunt like that again," says Kazu. "And if you do, tell me first." He grabs some throw pillows from the couch and hands them to me. "And just for that, you can sleep on the couch tonight."

"You're not serious," I say.

"Oh, but I am. I am quite serious, Husband."

"Hope is the force underlying much of human endeavor -- bearing children, saving money, sowing crops, building bridges, playing the lottery, falling in love. Hope is inextricably bound up with the future."

-- A Biologist's View of Hope
Vaughn Edgington

JADA

27. FAMOUS

When *Psychology Tomorrow* interviews me at the Drake Hotel, I feel like a spokesperson. Kind of like the Jenny Craig lady, but without the calorie counting. Me, a spokesperson for anything? It's new to me, but then everything is new to me these days.

As a native Chicagoan, I'm used to adapting to changes in the world around me. But I'm less familiar with adapting to changes in the world within me. Chicagoans know how 100-degree summers can turn senior citizens into statistics; how arctic winters with their five-foot-high snow drifts can change highways into parking lots. We've adapted not only to harsh weather but to great changes of all kinds. When Oprah moved her Harpo Studios empire out of Chicago, we did not crumble. We wished her well and moved on. When Illinois governors, one by one, were marched off to prison for racketeering or extortion, we shrugged our shoulders but still put on our Capri pants one leg at a time.

But for the past five decades, my life has had no unexpected twists and turns. That is, until now. On this one particular winter day, I remember walking into Barnes & Noble, heading straight for the magazine racks. At first, I don't see the issue so I ask for assistance. "Hi, do you know if you have the latest issue of *Psychology Tomorrow?*" I ask.

And that's when the clerk points to it. There I am staring back down at me. My radiant face. Thank god for Photoshop. Did I lose weight? I look amazing. I look around but no one seems to notice. I grab five copies of the magazine and head for the check-out line. I'm wondering if the clerk will recognize me from the cover. But there is a line of customers and he makes no connection, punches the keys on the register and slides my card through.

"It's me," I say to him shyly.

"Excuse me?" he says.

"On the cover. That's me."

Now he looks at the magazine. His eyes widen. "Oh my gosh! Can I have an autograph?" This the first time anyone has asked for my autograph. I kind of like it.

When The Hope Store opened shop, I don't think Chicago was prepared for the impact the store would have. Even the hope guys admit they underestimated the love -- and the hate – that the store would inspire. This store has become a very big thing. Throughout the Chicagoland area, in coffeehouses, at dinner tables, in therapy sessions, at water coolers -- brand-new conversations are just getting started about hope. Where does hope come from, how do you make more of it, do I need some?

The electronic footprint that Kazu and Luke share has grown geometrically in a matter of months. There are rumors that CNN just might want to host the first-ever Town Hall Meeting on Hope. Now that would make for some fine TV viewing.

As I move through the orbit of my life, I sense there may be something new inside of me. I stroll down Clark Street past Sir Spa, past the cute coffeehouses, keeping my eyes peeled for whatever comes my way. I am prepared to calibrate even the most microscopic changes in my life. But because I am still essentially me, I am also totally prepared for failure, for disappointment on an epic scale. Only when I'm positive that no one is nearby do I dare whisper to myself: "Hope for something, Jada. Hope for anything."

Otis and I have watched as the city has broken into different camps on the topic of man-made hope. It's the Natural Hopers vs. the Enhanced Hopers. What some view as groundbreaking, inspiring or evolutionary -- others view as unnatural, controversial or outright dangerous.

But it is too damn late. The genie, as they say, is out of the bottle.

It can never be put back inside the bottle again. Hallelujah for that.

I climb into bed tonight, but my heart isn't in it. My heart is elsewhere. I toss and turn. I get up and raid the fridge. Gobble what's left of some pecan pie I brought home from Razon. I watch CNN for a few minutes. I turn off the light and toss and turn.

Repeat.

This goes on for over an hour. Surely this is part of the excitement of the night: Kazu showing my brain scan lit up like Mardi Gras. The idea that a national magazine would want to interview me for their cover story! There's a fairy tale feeling in the air tonight and it's not just from the wine Kazu and I toasted with. So I'm trying my best to fall asleep but it ain't happening.

I don't exactly go to sleep but at some point, I must have waved the white flag because I am aware that my eyes are closed and I feel like I'm sleeping, but I also notice a cold draft. *When I open my eyes, I see the streetlights along Marine Drive and some stray cars. I sit up, dazed and frightened to realize I am outdoors, lying on the cold concrete of my fifteenth-floor balcony.*

I have no idea how I got here. I pick myself up off the concrete floor. I reach to open the sliding glass door. It's locked. I push harder on the door but it doesn't budge. *Where is my cell phone?* Through the glass, I see it's inside on my desk where it's supposed to be. I'm cold and dressed in sweats. *What do I do now?* I look down below at a cold Chicago day; no one is out strolling.

"Hello?! Can anyone hear me?" I shout to any neighbors who might hear me.

Nothing.

I can either stay on the balcony and catch my death of cold, or I can break the sliding glass door. After half an hour, I make my decision. I pick up a big ceramic flower pot. I never really liked it anyway.

My first attempt is feeble and bounces off the glass. But my second attempt shatters the door. I fall forward upon shards of glass. It's only later when I'm making myself a cup of tea that I realize it: I'm bleeding. And I can't make it stop.

Later I realize this is my first major side effect from the hope installation: sleepwalking. Reading the brochures closer, I see that the amazing benefits of the hope installation may be accompanied by a truckload of nasties of which sleepwalking is just one.

Luke shares with me that out of 682 clinical subjects over a three-year period, 78 subjects experienced the lesser side effects. One subject suffered a serious stroke and one committed suicide. And while it couldn't be proven for sure these side effects were connected to their installations, a red flag was raised. So they added them to the list of possible side effects.

I am concerned, but not totally freaked out. After all, lots of modern medicines list awful possible side effects on their labels, but we take them anyway.

No one ever said that life in the new millennium was perfect.

And no one ever will.

JADA

28. FANCY PEOPLE

Otis and I are in the emergency room of Weiss Memorial on this chaotic fall day. He insisted I see a doctor. I've got some cuts from the broken glass but nothing that won't heal. Thanksgiving was just last week and already there are holiday decorations everywhere. A handful of nurses in Santa hats strolls by wearing blinking Christmas light necklaces. In the ER lobby, there are people hacking and coughing, a little boy scratching a rash on his arm, an array of patients with secret ailments.

"How did you lock yourself out on the balcony?" Otis asks me as he hands me a paper cup filled with bad vending machine coffee.

"Aren't you forgetting the other question?" I say. "Like what was I doing on the balcony in the middle of the night in the first place?"

"Okay."

"Otis, all I know is I went to bed last night…and when I woke up I was lying on my balcony. I think I was sleepwalking."

"You've never sleepwalked before," he says.

"I've never had a hope installation before either. They said it's one possible side effect."

He sips his own bad coffee and makes a face. "In that case, maybe you better sleep with your cell phone in your pocket."

"And I better figure out a way to permanently lock the balcony door. Maybe I could sleep over at your place for a few nights."

"Maybe."

An intoxicated man enters the lobby dressed in a Santa suit and slowly takes a seat opposite us. He stares at me and waves a large candy cane in my direction, but I am totally not in the mood.

"The doctor will patch you up and you'll be good as new," Otis says. "How you feeling?"

"I still can't believe I'm the cover girl for *Psychology Tomorrow*! Can you?"

"Yes, I can," he says. "You have a story to tell. You are starting to go places, Jada. Exciting places. I wish I could…go with you."

"Now what's that supposed to mean?"

"Nothing," he says. "I'm just talking nonsense." I sense that Otis is happy for me, but there's also sadness.

Then he says, "You're changing. You're coming into your own. I guess you're spreading your hope wings, so you're going to be moving in new circles."

"What exactly are you trying to say, Otis Franklin?"

"I'm just saying I am not a fancy man. Never have been; never will be. So if you meet someone else…someone that travels in your new circle…"

I shake my head. "You're right about one thing. You are talking a whole lotta nonsense."

"I'm just saying, don't let me hold you back." Otis doesn't look at me when he says this. Then the receptionist calls my name so we can't continue our discussion. I go in to see the doctor alone.

The doc tends to my cuts and tells me how to change the bandages, but honestly I'm not hearing a word he's saying. I'm thinking of Otis sitting in the lobby and how he says I'm changing. I can tell part of him is happy for me, for my new hope, and part of him is very, very sad. But I know that I'm still Jada Upshaw. I don't think the installation changed me so much as it *revealed* me. Kind of like the way a sculptor creates a sculpture of a person, not by adding to the block of stone but by chipping away at it.

If sleepwalking is a side effect of my installation, I have to wonder what other side effects I might have to look forward to. How many others can I endure? But if my hope levels remain promising, what choice do I have? I decide to call Kazu and Luke for their guidance. I will have Otis drive me to The Hope Store straight from the hospital.

· ★ ·

At the store, I introduce Otis to the hope boys.

"Sleepwalking is a possible side effect, but it only affected 2% of our research subjects," says Kazu.

"Lucky me," I say.

"Before the sleepwalking, Jada also said she was having hallucinations," says Otis. "We didn't connect it to the hope installation at the time."

"In the middle of one night, I heard someone in my kitchen," I say. It freaked me out. When I walked into the kitchen, I saw my niece Angie sitting at the table eating a turkey dinner by candlelight. She looked at me and picked up a carving knife. I thought she was going to attack me but then she dropped the knife to the floor. I bent down to pick it up and when I stood up – she was gone."

Otis shakes his head. "That sounds like something straight out of a movie. Jada, you're too much. That's all there is to it."

"Hallucinations are a possible side effect," Luke says. "Again, it's very rare."

"So what do you guys think I should do?" she asks.

"I think we should see how things go over the next week," says Luke. "I don't want to do an extraction unless it's absolutely necessary."

"I totally agree," says Kazu. "We don't want to over-confuse the brain. There have only been four instances where people asked for hope extractions during the trial period. In two cases, the subjects returned to their original hope levels but never surpassed them. In the third case, the subject says his hope level was actually lower than when he started."

I give a look to Otis. "Okay, that's three. So what about the fourth subject?"

Kazu hesitates a moment and looks at Luke. "He's no longer with us," Luke says.

LUKE

29. A TINY PAPER WORLD

The cover story on Super Responder Jada hits just days before her sleepwalking episode. And what should have been a high point in Jada's life has morphed into something else. She feels like a fraud. Business at The Hope Store, however, has never been better. It's crazy good. We are booked solid for the next several months and Kazu and I are seriously talking about hiring new staff to help absorb the increased caseload. The investors have breathed a collective sigh of relief for the first time since we opened.

Today Kazu and I take a break from the store to do some holiday shopping. The mayor has lit the immense holiday tree in Millennium Park and the stores downtown have been playing Christmas music since the start of November. I've dropped a lot of hints that I really wouldn't mind being given one of those fancy Keurig coffee machines with a flavorful assortment of coffee pods. And I'm still trying to figure out what I should get for Kazu, but I know he's really happy with anything I get him. He's not materialistic at all. As long as we can spend quality time together and eat delicious food and talk. Mostly, we just like to talk. From the moment we met, Kazu and I have always felt so comfortable together. That may not seem like a big thing to most people, but it's big to us.

I'm glad that our chat with Jada has persuaded her to hold off on the hope extraction. The procedure is much more experimental than the hope installation. Jada should just rest for a while and see how things go. I call her and tell her I'd like to stop by her house if that's okay. She says it's okay. I generally like to keep some boundaries between a client and myself but urgent situations call for urgent measures. I want to see with my own eyes where she lives and more importantly *how* she lives these days since her side effects have begun.

When Jada opens the door, nothing prepares me for what I see.

There are dioramas filling up every square inch of her place, little story boxes blocking out any available light, dioramas hanging from strings that turn like mobiles when you breathe on them, dioramas on every available surface. I can't walk anywhere without stepping on a tiny paper world.

"Don't you love them?" she asks, admiring her handiwork.

"Wow, Jada," I say. "I'm speechless. I literally don't know what to say."

"I owe it all to The Hope Store," she says. Her eyes are huge, searching. "As a young girl, I was fascinated by dioramas. They were like mini-museums. It occurred to me that I needed to create a diorama to commemorate every significant moment of my life. To really bear witness to them, you know?"

What I know is this: something is not right.

I slowly take in all that is before me. Each diorama is clearly titled: "Getting fired from my last job." "Willis and Angie being born." "Meeting Otis for the first time." "Getting molested by Uncle Robbie." "My most recent, fumbled suicide attempt." "Momma lying in her coma." "Having my first hope installation."

I nod my head in appreciation. "It's very creative, Jada. But I must be honest. I'm a little concerned…"

"Don't you like them, Luke? I haven't been this creative in years. I'm positively prolific!" she says.

"Maybe we should look into the hope extraction after all," I suggest.

"You said I should wait and see how things go."

"Things are more serious than I thought."

"Really?" she says as if that's the last thing she thought I'd say. "But if you let me keep my new hope a while longer, I can be your new Ambassador of Optimism. I can go to cancer wards and grant last wishes to dying children..."

I survey her home. There's not a square inch that is not uncovered, no place for me to even sit down. "Jada, where do you sleep?"

She laughs. "Sleep? Who has time to sleep with all this work I have to do?"

"Let me help you clear some space on your bed," I say, carefully lifting some dioramas to a shelf already crammed with stuff. I study Jada's face, her flickering eyes, her twitchy body language. "Just think about the hope extraction, Jada. Sleep on it," I say.

But in my mind I'm whispering, "Oh my god. What have we done to this poor woman?"

QUANDARY

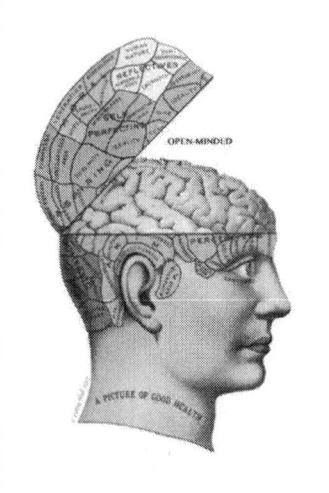

"I'm through watching test patterns on TV.
I want to dance on the dining room table
like everyone else."

-- from the poem "Letters I Never Wrote"

174

JADA

30. WIDE AWAKE

I go to bed tonight, sipping a hot cup of apple cider so there is warmth flowing through my body. I picture the cider flowing down my throat and arriving at my stomach. My belly feels warm. I turn on the wave machine and am serenaded by ocean waves. For a change, sleep comes easily to me.

In the middle of the night, I look at the clock: it's 3 a.m. When I roll over, I'm startled to see someone lying in bed next to me, looking right at me. It's a woman. *Huh? Am I dreaming?* Then the woman sits bolt upright in bed. She's me! She's my mirror image.

"Hi, I'm from your parallel universe. You can just call me Jada2," says the woman.

"Excuse me?"

"I must have slipped through a membrane or something. Stranger things have happened."

I'm scared. I've never had an intruder in my house. "I'm going to call the police. I have a gun," I lie.

175

She laughs. "Everyone's got a gun these days. You think that makes you special? Please, this is Chicago. The Wild MidWest. And the police? Parallel universes are out of their jurisdiction, I assure you." She laughs. "We don't even have donuts where I come from."

I study her face. She's a pretty, black woman. She definitely has my eyes. I'd recognize those windows of the soul anywhere. Her manner is alert but guarded. And she's wearing the same blue-green pajamas I'm wearing.

"Are you really from my parallel universe?" I ask, more fascinated than frightened.

"I'm sorry for dropping in like this. I'll be on my way." She closes her eyes and puts her hands together as if praying.

"Wait, what's it like...over there?"

She smiles. "In your parallel world, you finally get your hope levels together. In your parallel world, the love you take is equal to the love you make. In your parallel world, there are no side effects whatsoever."

I smile back. "Do you think I'd like it there?"

"Well, I like it. And I'm you."

I think for a minute. Something doesn't make sense. "Wait a minute. You said there are no side effects in your world. But aren't you a side effect from my installation?"

"Gotta run, sweetie. If you make it to the other side, let's do coffee." The woman turns into a cloud of silver confetti and blows away.

I look at the clock again: it's 2 a.m. How is it possible it's earlier now? I close my eyelids. When I open them, I am in high school taking drivers ed. It's the last time I was behind the wheel of a car.

"Make sure you can tell the difference between the brake and the gas pedal," says my instructor. I turn to see his face. It's Blair Matters. "Don't look at me. Keep your eyes on the road or you're going to get us both killed."

"Aren't you Blair Matters?" I say.

"What's it *to* ya?" he snaps.

"But I didn't know you in high school."

"Since when do dreams make sense?" he says.

I blink my eyelids again and when I open them, I'm sitting in a Mini-Cooper at a Shell gas station. But this doesn't feel like a dream. It feels real. It's night time. The motor is running. How did I get here? Blair is nowhere to be seen. Am I sleep-walking? Sleep-driving? A car behind me starts honking. What am I doing driving a car? I haven't had a license since high school. I climb out of the car, begging the other driver for patience. Then I make a mad dash and eventually flag down a cab. I make it home. I lock the door behind me.

I look at my bed. Once again, I see someone under the covers.

"Back so soon," says Jada2.

I reach for my cell and dial Luke. I look at the clock: it's 1 a.m. The phone rings and rings.

"Hello," says a groggy Luke Nagano.

"Luke, I'm so sorry to call so late. But it's an emergency." I tell him what's been happening. That weird shit like this has been happening all week and I don't think I can take it anymore. I'm ready to try the hope extraction. He says to meet him at The Hope Store right now. Kazu will help with the procedure.

Luke once told me according to Japanese legend, when you can't sleep at night it's because you're awake in someone else's dream. That would explain a lot.

Otis drives me to the store. When we get there, Luke and Kazu greet us.

"I'm so sorry this is happening to you," says Kazu. He embraces me.

Together the four of us walk down the dark corridor toward the Installation Suite. When we arrive Kazu says, "So the hope extraction is a way to un-do the hope installation. It should remove the side effects, but will also remove the good effects. It returns you to your pre-installation hope level. It's a way to re-boot. The dopamine will slowly leave your receptors."

"My hope juice," I say. I look at Otis to see his reaction. He nods with great concern.

"I don't mind some minor side effects, but these side effects are huge. I can't live like this, Kazu," I say. "Let's do it."

Kazu moves to a control panel and pushes some levers.

Luke guides me to take a seat under the equipment. "Do you have any questions before the extraction begins? Once we start, we can't stop. There's no going back," Luke says.

"Well, of course I have a million questions but now is not the time for questions. Now is the time for action."

Luke smiles. "Just take some deep breaths, Jada. Here we go." He nods to Kazu.

Kazu pulls a red lever forward slowly.

Just as before, a beam of light encircles my head like a luminous blue lampshade.

The light radiates a cool temperature in the room. As I look outward at the suite, everything shimmers in the blue light as if underwater.

Suddenly there is a sharp pain in my head and I wince. I reach up with one hand to rub my head.

Everyone notices. "Are you okay, Jada?" Kazu asks.

I massage my forehead with the tips of my fingers.

"It's best not to touch your head during the extraction. If you're feeling any discomfort, it should pass very soon," says Kazu.

The pain subsides and I lower my hand.

And now silver dots of confetti magically rise up. They float upward in graceful, slow motion.

It looks like it's snowing in reverse.

On the far wall, I watch in a mirror as the confetti seems to pass through a membrane in my head till it all disappears. The room returns to normal.

"How are you feeling?" says Luke?

"I'm fine. Just a little...woozy."

"Just sit tight for a while," he says. "I'll get you some water. You did great."

Kazu runs an fMRI on me to check my levels and sure enough I have reverted to this walnut shell of a brain with a glimmer of yellow light along one hemisphere. This makes me very sad, but I say nothing. I don't want to appear ungrateful for all the work Kazu has done.

"Oh," says Kazu, "we should remind you that next week, CNN is hosting a town hall meeting on hope. You're welcome to attend, but we also understand if you'd rather not. The most important thing now is for you to regain your equilibrium.

There's always the chance that the brain might naturally re-hardwire itself, but this is all new territory. To tell you the honest truth, Jada -- 95% of any scientific discovery is pure science. But that last 5%? It's a mystery. It's magic. I use my Buddhist chanting for that last 5% that I can't figure out with my college-educated mind. That's where a leap of faith comes in handy."

And it isn't until Kazu lays it out like this that I really know what he means. Science doesn't know everything. There are things that happen in the world that are magic, that even science can't explain...or explain away. That's a good thing and a bad thing too.

JADA

31. PRE-HEATED

I do my volunteer shift at the animal shelter, but my heart isn't in it. Ever since the hope extraction, it's like a veil has come down over me. I go back to the few routines I have in search of something familiar, something comforting.

Later I'm off to Sheila's house to babysit Willis and Angie. Sheila and hubby are off for a little "them time."

Willis, Angie and I are in the kitchen making sugar cookies. Or to be more precise: I am making sugar cookies, Angie is stirring the batter but spilling batter too, and Willis attempts to lick the spoon when I'm not looking. The oven is pre-heating. I picture the molecules in the oven speeding up their vibrations. I like the sigh of a gas oven, the warmth filling the kitchen. It reminds me of something else, something thrilling and troubling -- but I can't remember what it is.

"When I grow up, Aunt Jada, can I be a princess? I'd live in my own castle, but you can visit sometime."

I crack a few eggs on the Formica counter and drop the gooey contents into the batter.

I'm about to say something inappropriate. I can just feel it. In spite of all my heartfelt promises to my sister. I can't help myself.

"Angie, you know how I usually say you can be whatever you want to be? No matter how impossible it may seem?" She nods and stirs.

"That's not really true."

"Were you telling a fib?"

"Something like that. See, the truth is the chance of you becoming a princess is less than 1%. You have to be born into a racket like that. Plus, you're black, which doesn't help at all." I scan the recipe book for the next step. *Add 2 cups of sugar. Stir vigorously. Stir as if your life depended on it.*

"I just want to grow up and be happy," says my niece, a tear forming in the corner of one eye. She wipes it away.

"Ha! Good luck with that. You've got better chances of becoming a princess. You think my grown-up friends are happy? The happiest time of your life, Angie, is right now when you're small and have no responsibilities. The older you get, the harder it gets." I feel this irresistible urge to extinguish the tiny flame of hope that burns inside this small human.

I fill the measuring cup with sugar. I grind the sugar into the batter with a wooden spoon.

Willis chimes in. "You shouldn't say stuff like that to her. Or she'll never want to grow up," he says. Then he adds, "My mother says you're sick. Upstairs." He points to his head. "Is that true?

"Probably. I have my good days and my bad days."

"How did you get sick?" Willis asks me. And it's such a simple question, but there is no simple answer.

Angie takes over stirring the batter in the bowl.

"I'm not sure I can really explain it."

"I think Mommy's sick too, Aunt Jada," says Willis.

"Why do you say that, sweetie?"

"Because she cries a lot and she always tells Daddy, *You make me sick*. Why does Daddy want to make Mommy sick?" Angie has lost all interest in sugar cookies, has forgotten what has brought the three of them into the kitchen in the first place. She wanders out of the kitchen to who knows where.

"Let's just focus on baking our treats. How about that?" I tell Willis. I start spooning little mounds of dough onto the baking sheet, mashing them flat. Spooning and mashing. Spooning and mashing.

"Do you think my parents are happy?" asks Willis. I spoon and mash, uncertain what to say.

Willis sits down on a chair. "It doesn't matter. Everything is stupid and when you grow up -- it gets stupider."

I give the boy my full attention. "Willis, I'm just a mixed-up girl. Always have been, always will be. Ignore everything I said. Soon we'll have warm cookies with milk and everything will be better."

"Whatever," he says, not even looking at me. I grip the baking sheet and slide it into the oven. When the oven door slams shut, Angie wanders back into the kitchen.

"The cookies will be done in about fifteen minutes," I say. "You know this little talk we had tonight? Let's pretend it never happened, okay? It'll be our little secret." The children look at me with blank expressions like unfinished dolls at a toy factory.

"Why don't you kids watch TV? I'll let you know when they're ready." The kids don't have to be told twice to go watch TV. What has gotten into me? Such a heavy conversation. Could it be side effects from the hope extraction? The smell of freshly baking cookies wafts through the kitchen and erases any trace of sadness. Life is simple again.

Sheila and hubby arrive. Delicious cookie smells fill the air. I take the pan out and put it on the stove.

I leave, not even bothering to take a cookie with me.

:★:

At home, I'm just settling in to watch a movie on Netflix when the phone rings. I let it ring a few times as I grab hold of the remote and sip a frosty glass of Diet Dr. Pepper.

"Hey Sheila," I say.

"Don't 'hey Sheila' me," she says.

"Is something wrong?"

"What in the world have you been talking to my children about? What crazy ideas are you putting into their heads now?"

"Wow, they couldn't keep that secret for more than half an hour. That's a world record."

"Jada, I thought --" Sheila says.

"Look, there is nothing I said to those kids that, in my heart of hearts, I don't believe to be true. They were asking me big life questions. Was I supposed to lie?"

"If the questions are that big, let them talk to their Mommy and Daddy. You're not their Momma. You're barely my sister!"

"Excuse me?"

"I didn't mean that," says Sheila, though she knows no amount of back peddling will save her.

"Is that what you really feel?"

"It's just that...well, with you being depressed for so much of --"

"I'm not depressed. I'm hope-challenged."

"Same difference."

"No. No, it's not."

"Jada, you haven't always been fully present for me. Not even for yourself. And now that you got this fancy new hope installed, and all the reporters want to talk to you...you're even less present."

"So I'm not supposed to have a little hope and glamor in my life? Is that it?"

"You know I want you to be happy."

We both pause for a moment. On the phone, all that can be heard are cartoons in the background. Angie is entertaining herself as the theme song for "Dora, the Explorer" plays in the distance.

Sheila and I are explorers too. Explorers in a lonely galaxy with no maps to guide us.

"I'm sorry, Sheila. I don't know how I got into that conversation, but once I was there, it was hard to get out." I say, wishing I had a cookie about now. "I recently had a hope extraction. Maybe it has something to do with that."

"When are you going to stop blaming everything on this hocus-pocus and start taking some responsibility?" Sheila collects her thoughts. "Look, I've got to get to bed soon. We're coming up on a new year, Jada. Time to start the year right. I love you, but you can't talk to the kids like you talked to them tonight. Kids are like sponges, they absorb whatever you pour into them. Let them be kids for a while."

"Last time I checked, they were still kids."

"You know what I mean." Sheila is getting frustrated. "If we can't agree on this, I won't be able to let you babysit them anymore. Is that what you want?"

"It doesn't seem to matter much what I want, Sheila," I say. "You're going to do what you want to do anyway. You always do." And I hang up.

My hope levels are stalled, for now, so I switch gears to Plan B. It's time to do more research on what I call my "Exit Strategy." Truth is, I didn't really expect much from The Hope Store. I expected to be disappointed which I was. A self-fulfilling prophecy. I must make preparations, research alternatives.

So I am getting my affairs in order, as they say. I've typed up a sheet of all my computer passwords – for my laptop, utility bills, bank accounts, credit cards, websites, etc. I have prepared a last will and testament. I'll leave most things to Otis and Sheila. Sheila will be the executor of my will and have medical power of attorney. In my living will, I've made it crystal clear that no heroic measures are to be taken to sustain my life. *If only heroic measures had been taken to LIVE my life*, I think to myself. I want to be cremated and to have my ashes scattered. No funeral, no memorial, no obituary.

I just want to disappear.

What to do with my diaries? Destroy them? Put them all in a box and have a bonfire? Or leave them to be read like tea leaves scattered in a porcelain cup? I decide to destroy them. Why hurt people from the grave? I suffered once by living this life. Why make anyone suffer a second time by reading about it?

I continue to explore the various ways I can end my life. I have created a chart to help me compare and contrast different exit strategies based on various criteria: effectiveness, pain, messiness, costliness, popularity. For instance, hanging is inexpensive but painful and clearly not as foolproof as the data indicated. Pills are very popular, but can be costly and can result in coma or brain damage.

Google is the suicidal gal's best friend.

I do a search under "bathtub electrocution" because it sounds quick. You just lie in a tub of warm water and lowering a boom box playing pretty music into the tub. Electrocution would be instant and affordable.

There's an article online from the UK where they look at 41 cases of death by bathtub electrocution in the previous year. The details are fascinating. 19 are men. 22 are women. The average age is fifty-one. 38 victims are in tubs filled with water. Interestingly, some are in bathtubs without water. Hmm. Electrical devices used: hair dryers, stereos, electric heaters, table lamps, electric fans. (One determined person used no less than THREE hair dryers!) I like the idea of using a boom box because it can play nice music too. Six deaths are deemed accidental.

Most victims are not dressed, though one victim is fully dressed in a tuxedo. I would rather not be found nude. Some of the bodies have a "cutaneous electric mark." That is a pale line around the body caused by the electricity corresponding to the water level in the tub at the time of death.

Only 11 out of 41 leave suicide notes letters. Most do not. Fascinating. Am I morbid? Okay, then I'm morbid.

I cut and paste this article into a Word document, tuck it away in a secret folder for a rainy day.

Lastly, I have written a final letter to Otis Franklin, my partner of many years. On the outside of the envelope is a note that the letter is to be read after my death.

LUKE

32. WHEN YOU BELIEVED

Sometimes I get so caught up with Jada's case that I forget about all the amazing success stories we've had already here at the store. Maybe it's because Jada was my first customer, or because she was our first Super Responder client. She became a symbol for people. Installing hope in her was like turning on a light switch. And then the dreaded side effects came. At The Hope Store, we measure success by three criteria.

1. ANECDOTAL PROOF -- Do the clients tell us they feel more hopeful? How do the clients feel about their goals, the future? Do they feel more empowered and excited about them? What changes are noticed by their peers?

2. BEHAVIORAL PROOF -- What new actions are the clients able to take in pursuit of their goals? Do they take concrete steps toward making their goals come true? Do the clients find they are able to take actions that they haven't been able to take in the past?

3. SCIENTIFIC PROOF -- An fMRI is done to monitor any changes in dopamine levels. This confirms that new channels to receive dopamine have been opened up in the brain, as a result of the intended brain confusion. The clients receive color print-outs of their before and after brain scans.

There is the case of Dora, a fussy, middle-aged woman in middle management. Her inability to hope created a kind of glass ceiling all its own that had nothing to do with gender or age. It was self-imposed. She supervised an accounting department for a major music label, but secretly wanted to be a recording artist herself. Years of therapy didn't help. She was hopeless, not merely depressed, and there was no medication for that. And then Dora came to The Hope Store and everything changed. After her installation, her brain started to process hope differently. She pictured herself stepping away from her desk at work, away from her fax machine and her Blackberry. She pictured herself stepping closer and closer to a live microphone under a bright spotlight...opening her mouth...and singing.

She hasn't quit her day job, but she's gone part-time and she's hard at work on her first demo in a recording studio. She's hopeful.

There are cases of people who've isolated themselves socially because of their condition, people who wanted love but had no faith in their ability to achieve it. All these people reported a surge in hope levels that enabled them to move closer toward their goals.

To be fair, we have had dissatisfied customers too. Some people reported no change in their hope levels -- anecdotally or behaviorally. Then we'd do a brain scan to check for scientific evidence of improvement. Sometimes there'd be a marked increase in dopamine levels, but the customer could not perceive it.

And many times people came to the store with warped ideas about what hope was. They thought that The Hope Store would cause all their dreams to come true. We have never made such a guarantee. Hope awakens one's courage and passion to pursue their dreams, but ultimately it's up to the person to do the work. Hope is the engine, but you are still driving the car. It is your foot on the accelerator.

Overall business has been very good. Clients who have good hope responses tend to tell their peers which results in referrals. As always, the things that people hope for are diverse. Here are a few of the hopes of our current clients: win the lottery, washboard abs, save our home from foreclosure, have a healthy baby, build a wall, build a bridge, make my malignant tumor turn benign, get a green card, talk to the dead, make contact with aliens, and so on.

We don't judge. That's not our job.

An article appears in Chicago magazine. "It's neither a puff piece nor a hatchet job," I say to Kazu." It talks about The Hope Store in a way that is surprisingly balanced." Kazu looks on as I read part of it aloud:

"The Hope Store, Revisited"
by Blair Matters

Special to Chicago Magazine

The Hope Store has been open for a month now. I thought I'd stop by and see how business is going. There have been protestors against artificial hope since day one. The passion of the naysayers is matched only by the passion of the store's advocates.

What is the difference between hope and hype? In the case of The Hope Store which claims to install new hope in the hope-challenged — not a whole lot. Nestled in the heart of trendy Andersonville, one of Chicago's more bohemian neighborhoods, this shop is in the perfect location for the boomer crowd that frequents this hood.

I recently camped out in the lobby of the store so that I could speak candidly with customers, past and present, disgruntled and hopeful. The annual procedure costs $1,000 but they're offering an introductory special of $750 for now. The procedure is not currently covered by insurance. It's pricey *to be sure, and not easily afforded by the unemployed and the poor.*

The "hope installation" is a process which combines a powerful magnetic field and a slow-falling, metallic confetti-like substance. The neurological effect of this? It essentially tricks the brain into manufacturing more dopamine. Dopamine is a neurotransmitter sometimes referred to as "the chemical of anticipation" as it is released right before hope is experienced.

<u>Said one unhopeful customer</u>: *"You shell out all the money but you get nothing tangible in return. I felt some glimmers of something, but nothing worth that kind of money. I thought once I got my dose of hope, I'd get everything I hoped for. That has not been the case for me. I am very disappointed."*

<u>Said one hope-filled customer</u>: *"Frankly, I thought $750 was cheap. That's barely ten hours with a shrink, and you know how little happens in ten hours with a shrink! For me, the treatment activated all the affirming voices in my head, and I was able to hear for the first time the true voice of my own hope. I felt like a slave who's been unshackled. I've recommended the store to my friends and they're all having terrific results."*

<u>Said Kazu Mori</u>, the developer of the hope installation process: *"We see people transformed before our eyes at The Hope Store. It's not just that their thinking changes; their lives change. How much of that is placebo effect vs. the effect of the hope installation? Hard to say. But as*

long as the customer is living more dynamically, does it matter? Our rational minds tell us there needs to be a black-and-white answer, but our souls don't really care. Our souls just want joy, hope, more love. Even if we can't rationally explain to ourselves how we got there. We don't just instill hope at The Hope Store. We install it. And to do that we tap into three different worlds: the world of biotechnology, the world of pure faith, and the world of our own unshakable happiness.

Biotechnology as I understand it acknowledges there is no separation between body and mind. None whatsoever. When I refer to the world of faith, I don't mean religion. I mean the true faith you had as a child when you believed in the possibility of everything. When you believed in yourself."

I send a copy of the article to my printer. Kazu looks at me expectantly. "I knew there was a reason why I married you." At just that moment, an email appears in my in box.

It's from Blair Matters.

· ★ ·

Blair sits across the table from us at Starbucks. "I know somebody who knows somebody who used to work at CNN," he says. "That person passed along my message that CNN's coverage of the hope installation phenomenon had been stellar, but that the subject of modern hope was so big and so important, it cried out for a town hall meeting. I told them I would love to moderate such an event. To my surprise, they emailed me back. They already had a town hall on hope in the works, but their guy Andrew Konstant was slated to moderate. They agreed to let me sit on a panel with you folks. Would you be up for that?"

"Wow, a town hall meeting? That sounds major," says Luke.

"What's the catch?" Kazu says.

Blair smiles. "No catch. Just show up and answer a few questions. You get tons of free advertising on a high profile media event. What's not to like? It'll be a great chance to respond to the concerns of the Natural Hopers and find a common ground. Just have all your hope ducks in a row."

"Indeed," I say. I picture that row of ducks, and one duck falls over.

LUKE

33. LOVERS & LAWYERS

Kazu and I are going out to meet friends for a movie and dinner. It will be a much-needed break from the store. We are getting dressed and ready to go. He pulls on jeans and a blue thermal shirt. I pull on my brown corduroys and a gray sweatshirt that says "Obey" on the front.

"Don't get me wrong, Kazu, I think the town hall is a fantastic opportunity. But I also don't trust Blair. There's no telling what questions might come up," I say.

Kazu pulls on a black cardigan. "He's a loose cannon."

"Kazu, have you ever wondered who the Natural Hopers really are?"

"They're tree-huggers who still churn their own butter," he says. "Very anti-science. They're probably vegan too."

"But if they're just a grassroots group, how the heck do they afford to do fancy TV spots and the fancy brochures?" I step into my slip ons and walk to my computer. "Check this video out."

On-screen is the image of a baby spinning gently through space.

The voiceover says: *"You were born perfect with the ability to hope. And there are natural things that you can do to keep that hope alive."* There is a stream of images that accompany the voiceover:

"Did you know physical exercise like running can increase your endorphins, a substance released in the brain resulting in a greater feeling of hopefulness? Did you know that the flower essence from the Gorse bush can revive hope in a person who has lost it? Did you know that cognitive therapy has transformed the psychotherapy world by allowing the individual to master his own mind, instead of his mind mastering him?"

Onscreen is an image of our store.

"There's a new store in town called The Hope Store that claims to install hope in the hopeless, but their procedures are still too new and invasive to be considered safe. It's $1,000 a year for treatment and no insurances currently cover it. Manage your hope supply naturally. Visit us at NaturalHopers.com to learn more about natural ways to restore your hope levels. Paid for by Natural Hopers United."

"Wow," when did they start running those? "Kazu asks.'

"Today. I did some digging," I say. "The Natural Hopers are funded by some big for-profits. This may come in handy at the town hall meeting." I also was curious what dirt they might dig up on us. I looked at articles about our clinical trials. It said that one trial subject committed suicide. Is that true?"

Kazu hesitates as if unsure how to respond. "Well, and please don't be offended by this, but...you're not a scientist."

"What does that mean?"

"Within the scientific community, there is an understanding of how to interpret data, and how to research what we call *outliers in a clinical trial.* An outlier is a negative result that lies outside the norm, and so must be investigated." Kazu rubs his hand across his mouth as if trying to make the words easier to say.

"So to you a volunteer's death is just an outlying piece of data? Wow," I can say. "Wow, wow."

"I didn't say that --"

At some point during this argument, it occurs to me that our relationship, our business...might not survive this night. Kazu continues to defend his decision. "It's not just that I was afraid what the FDA would do. It's that the whole procedure...this beautiful, amazing opportunity...would be in jeopardy. Do you know how important a procedure this is? A scientist could wait their whole lifetime and never find something this big."

"There's a process in place. Why not trust it?" I ask.

"I can explain my thinking," Kazu says." But I'm not sure you'll understand."

"Try me." We lock the door and head for the car.

"As the sponsor of the clinical trial, The Hope Store is responsible for collecting outlier data for site investigators -- negative reactions, side effects, etc," he says. "But ultimately it's up to the sponsor's judgment as to whether these adverse events are reported as being related to the study treatment or not. We can allow for a certain amount of...*fluctuation* from the norm. Is it a conflict of interest? One could make that argument. But the FDA has ultimate oversight."

I'm scratching my head at this point. "So who decided on behalf of The Hope Store that the volunteer death should not be reported?"

"The fatality was reported. It was documented in the footnotes," he says. "And we do list suicidal impulses as a possible side effect."

I look at Kazu. "And who exactly made this final decision? Can't you just give me a straight answer?"

"The decision of how to interpret this data was made with input from our board," he says.

I take a breath because I need one. Then I say, "Well since we're clearing the air for the new year, I might as well share a secret of mine." Kazu looks up. "When I first came to LiveWell, I was part of the clinicals. I realized at one point that I wasn't having a big response to my installation."

"What are you talking about?" Kazu says. "You were one of the first Super Responders."

"Right. Well, what I wanted to tell you is that I *faked* my great response."

He looks up from his gadget. I have gotten his full attention, whether I want it or not.

"Because I wanted to stay part of the study, part of your life. I was afraid of losing you. So I pretended to be a Super Responder." I search Kazu's face for a reaction, but there is none forthcoming. "I imitated their physical behaviors, used words to describe my response that I'd heard Super Responders use. But now the store is open and I'm working with clients. They want me to talk about my own hope transformation – so I have to lie again. But I can't do it anymore."

Once again, I study Kazu's face. It is an inscrutable face.

"Say something," I say.

"You falsified trial data?" says Kazu.

"I know. I'm sorry. I did a terrible thing." Kazu stops talking. For a long time. We have dinner, watch the movie with friends. We drive home in silence.

When we get home, we silently get ready for bed. Like mimes.

On this cold winter night, I am the first one under the covers; Kazu strolls to bed with Kindle in hand. Neither of us speaks. I hate this feeling. We are acting like children.

"I guess we're not talking to each other," I say.

Kazu continues to read his e-book.

"That might work out better anyway," I say picking up my iPad. "That way I can play Angry

Birds and I won't have to listen to you *babble* about science all night."

Kazu does not look up once from his e-book device.

"Besides, we're both on Facebook," I continue. "If we have something really important to say, we can always private message each other." Surely he will crack a smile at that. I'm hoping for that smile. Nothing. Damn him.

Finally, Kazu cannot restrain himself any longer. "I do not babble."

"That's funny," I say. "I thought I heard a human voice in this empty bedroom. But how could that be? That breaks the laws of ordinary physics." But Kazu does not speak again. Sleep does not come easily

In the middle of the night, I can hear Kazu leave the bed. He goes into the living room to do some of his Buddhist chanting, very quietly.

The next morning when I wake up, I'm tempted to say good morning to Kazu. Then I remember we're not talking to each other. As I stir in bed, I can tell Kazu is also waking up. He stretches and yawns. Then he turns to face me. His face is open, smiling.

"For you information, I'm not mad at you," he says.

"You're not?"

"But I was. Goddammit, Luke, you falsified data for my study!" he shouts like a volcano that has just erupted. "How am I ever supposed to trust you again?"

"I did it because I didn't want to lose you. Are you hearing that part?"

"I hear it. But goddammit, Luke, you could've screwed up my FDA approval. Did that ever occur to you?" I'm nodding even before he finishes. I'm just glad Kazu is talking again. "Even worse, you could have prevented an amazing scientific breakthrough from reaching the people who need it the most."

"I thought if I was an Average Responder, I'd never see you again." I am getting emotional. I find my eyes watering. I wipe away some moisture from one eye. "It was stupid and I'm sorry."

He powers down his Kindle and puts it on the bed table, rubs his face with one hand as if to wipe away his weariness. "And you could've messed things up between us."

"So…tell me, why aren't you still mad at me?" I ask.

Kazu's face is close enough to kiss, but I restrain myself. "I couldn't sleep last night so at 3 a.m. I got up and emailed a colleague in Amsterdam who I'd worked with. She was my mentor," he says. "Of course, I pretended it was a hypothetical situation and no names were mentioned." Kazu walks over to the windows and raises the shades, letting the daylight in. Then he climbs back into bed.

"Anyway, I asked her what she would do if a volunteer falsified data as a way to appear more fascinating to her as a researcher, as a way to flirting -- what would she think about that? Before I could go further, she said if I wasn't absolutely flattered, then I've been spending way too much time staring into Petri dishes."

I lean over and kiss Kazu.

"Just because we have good hope levels doesn't mean we don't still have problems, right?" I say. Kazu just smiles.

"Amen to that, brother." He takes off his sweatshirt and I do likewise. We are shirtless. Our chests are smooth.

I look into Kazu's eyes. "I heard you chanting in the middle of the night."

"I'm sorry."

"Don't apologize. I like the sound," I say. "What were you chanting about?"

He looks deep into my eyes...like he could live there...behind my eyes. And I would let him. Oh yes, I would let him. "You," he says. "Us. Everything."

I interlace the fingers of my hand in his.

I press my bare chest against Kazu's back till we are perfect spoons in a drawer. When Kazu talks with his low John Wayne voice, I can feel his whole body vibrate like a drum.

"I hate to admit it, but I think your chanting worked," I say.

"It always does."

Outside I can hear the city is waking up, but I'm not ready to get out of bed. I play with Kazu's nipples which are hard. "I like that chanting is something done out loud," I say.

"Why?" he asks.

"Because I know when you're chanting, you're hoping for something."

When he laughs, his whole chest shakes. "Or maybe I'm like a cat and I'm purring."

"I wish people purred," I say, "so you could tell when they were happy." Kazu does a clumsy impression of a cat purr with his fluttering tongue like he's rolling his R's in Spanish class.

We move closer together for a major cuddling session. And then, as they say, we get busy.

JADA

34. A GOOD MAN

Otis is getting ready to leave. We're not done talking, but close enough. "The bottom line is: You don't appreciate me, Jada," he says. "You can see all kinds of goddam hallucinations, but you can't see the good man standing right in front of you. That's a damn shame. It really is." He starts to walk out. His eyes are tearing. I've never seen him cry before. "At first I wanted to end the relationship because I didn't want to hold you back from all the new people you are surely going to meet. But now I'm leaving because I don't know who you are anymore. I don't think you even care, Jada. You should care. Somebody should care." He continues to move toward the door.

"Otis Franklin, if you know nothing else about me, you should know that I care. I just don't always show it," I say. "I've been in my own little world lately. But I care about you, Otis. I do."

"I needed to hear that. But you're about five years too late." He gives a military salute. "Maybe I'll see you on the boulevard." He pulls the door closed.

I am tempted to run after him. But I don't. I just lean my back against the door. And the tears come. Lots of them.

The year is almost over.

A vow is a vow.

I know what I must do.

I cry because I came so close to finding hope. I really did. But close only counts in horseshoes. I sit down on a chair in the middle of the room, in the middle of a millennium, and I weep. I weep for both Jada's – the one I used to be, and the one I am becoming. And for Otis too. For sweet Otis, I weep too.

"In indigenous cultures, if you came to a medicine person complaining of hopelessness or dispiritedness -- they would ask three questions: When did you stop dancing? When did you stop singing? When did you stop hearing the beating of your own heart?"

-- Everyday Shamanism

JADA

35. ENCORE

I had thoroughly researched suicide by bathtub electrocution. I had my heart set on it. I was committed to it. I'd even bought a new hair dryer.

But today I nix the idea. I don't like the idea of my dead body wrinkling like a prune in the tub. Where's the dignity in that? And as intense as the hanging thing can be, it's so much quicker than pills, so much less messy than a gun. Besides, I'm determined to master death's learning curve. This time I have attached the hook to the ceiling with a huge anchor that supports up to two hundred fifty pounds. The helpful hardware man at Ace has assured me this hook would hold, would not give way like the last one.

I turn on the radio of my stereo. On a whim, I make a song request. I ask them to play "What's Going On" for me. The DJ makes a note of it and says he'll play it if he can squeeze it in. I thank him for everything he does for people. The songs, the requests, the encouragement.

I look at my neglected cat Shadow who sits on a window sill staring at me. I try to pet her but Shadow hisses at me. She never hisses. It's as if the cat knows what's going down and feels betrayed. I walk to the kitchen and open the cupboard, reach for a can of cat food and feed her. I reached into my purse and pull out my farewell letter to Otis. I never got around to rewriting it so this one will have to do. Then I grab my trusty can of spray paint and shake it vigorously. My last words. I think about how my sister called me a lifesaver. Nothing could be further from the truth:

I NEVER SAVED ANYONE'S LIFE.
NOT EVEN MY OWN.

Once again I lay down my wallet and keys on a kitchen table. I reach over to pet Shadow. I climb up onto the chair and place the leash around my neck.

The landline rings.

I let the answering machine get it: "Jada. Please pick up," says the voice. It's Otis. "I'm sorry. I don't know what got into me. I guess I have my bad days too. My damn company fired me today! Can you believe it? After twenty

years of loyalty and devotion? They're gonna do me
like that. I really want to talk to you. No, I really
need to talk to you. I was taking it out on you and
that wasn't right." There is a pause as if he's waiting
for a response. I undo the leash and step down
from the chair. I walk over and pick up the phone.

"Hi," I say.

"Hi," he says.

"I'm sorry you lost your job, Otis. And I'm
sorry about the way I talked to you. You're a good
man. There's an important letter here for you. Make
sure you read it, okay?" I say.

"Let's read it together. I love to read letters
out loud."

"Can't. I've got places to go. People to be. I
love you, Otis

"Take care. I've got to go." I hang up and
wipe my eyes. I glance up at my masterpiece of
graffiti on the wall.

I turn up the stereo in my living room. As I
step up onto the chair, the DJ cuts in: "This one
goes out to Jada who's having a rough time tonight.
Hang in there, sweetheart." And Marvin Gaye
croons "What's Going On?" But I don't know what's
going on anymore. Maybe I never did. I look at the
hook in the ceiling. I pray that it will hold.

I climb up onto the chair and put my neck
through the noose.

I hum along with Marvin Gaye.

I step off the chair.

And for one god-awful, terrifying moment, I dangle. I feel my windpipe slowly being crushed. Out of reflex, I kick my legs furiously but I feel life gradually leaving my body. It will all be over in a moment

And then there is the sound of a key jangling in the door.

"Oh my god!" he says. Otis runs to me, grabs my legs to lift me. He climbs up onto the chair and struggles to release the leash from my neck, but it's jammed. It won't open. With one arm supporting my full weight, he uses the other hand to try to work the leash. Finally, the leash gives and he pulls it from around my neck.

He brings me down and lies me on the sofa. "Jada! It's Otis. Breathe, baby! Hang in there, sweetheart." Nothing. Otis can't believe what's happening. His worst nightmare is coming true.

My body is just an empty container in his arms. I feel my spirit sadly, wearily rise up leaving its earthly container. I look down at Otis as he cradles me in his arms. My former body lies motionless, now without the breath of life.

And then I cough. Uh, that is, I mean my container coughs. I reach for my throat and rub it. "Why, Otis?" I manage to say. "Why did you do that?"

He is overjoyed. For a while, he rocks me gently as if I am a small child.

"I thought I lost you."

I try to speak, but for a moment I can't. It's just as well.

"I don't understand. I thought you were getting better," he says.

"I was better. I was great. But there were… complications," I say. "And right now I'm just sooo tired. You know what I mean, jelly bean? So if I don't see you again, I want you to find a woman and make a good life with her. Find someone normal."

Otis looks right into my eyes. "I don't want someone normal. I want *you.*"

And that touches me deeper than I can say. "Otis, Sweetheart, you can't have me. There's nothing left to have."

LUKE

36. PORTAL

Kazu and I take turns checking up on Jada. But in the days after her last suicide attempt, Otis reports she has mostly remained in bed sleeping at his place. This can't be a good sign. I call him once more. "Hi, Otis. How's sleeping beauty doing?"

"This is very weird but when I got home from work today, she wasn't in bed. She wasn't at my place at all," Otis says. "I hope she's not outside somewhere sleepwalking in rush hour traffic on Lakeshore Drive."

"Did you try calling her cell?" I ask.

"I did. She left her cell at my place. That's not like her."

:★·

A few days later, I get a call from her sister. Jada's turned up on Sheila's doorstep. She insists on keeping all the shades down so the reporters don't find her. "She's having disturbing nightmares," Sheila reports. "In the dreams, she says she enters a parallel world," says Sheila. "Her goal is to find the *portal* to the parallel world. She said Kazu would understand. Does any of this make sense to you?"

"Please tell her that these are only dreams and that she can wake up from them at any time. And tell her I am coming to see her right now," I say.

"Luke, this probably isn't the best time to say this but I've joined the Natural Hopers group. Robert Chang's not a bad guy."

"Sheila, you haven't."

"After seeing what my sister's gone through, -- I had to join. How is all this science helping her be a happier person? Every day she gets worse."

It's hard to hear this. "Don't give up hope. Once Jada hits bottom, there'll be nowhere to go but up. Kazu and I are exploring supplementary treatment. We're sifting through the clinical trial data for anything that might help your sister."

I am halfway to Sheila's house when my cell rings. It's Sheila. "Don't bother coming. She's disappeared again." And it's too late to search for Jada anyway. The town hall meeting is tomorrow. Kazu and I are going to practice posing questions to each other tonight over chicken teriyaki and bean pockets. And Chartreuse wants to do a conference call to make sure the investors have their say.

LUKE

37. A TOUGH ROOM

From the stage, I peer into the audience. So many people. The stage is appropriately festive with wreathes and twinkling lights, but not overly Christmassy. The energy tonight is both thrilling and terrifying. It's clear that the Natural Hopers will be well-represented in the audience and at the microphone. Local journalist Blair Matters who has been critical of our store will be on-hand as well. And with Jada missing again, there's no telling whether she'll make an appearance or not. That has me and Kazu on edge. Chartreuse was totally against her participating in any way. She was terrified the topic of her side effects would come up and that the Natural Hopers would jump on that band wagon. But Kazu and I didn't feel it was right to ask her *not* to come either. Surely there are other clients who can testify in support of the store. I doodle possible ideas for a December promotion as we wait for things to get underway,.

From somewhere just outside the auditorium, there is a commotion. I see footage of the disturbance on the huge video screens that surround us on stage. A chorus of protesters chants: "What do we want? HOPE! When do we want it? NOW!'"

And then there is another chorus of voices which replies with: "The Hope Store…is the Hype Store! The Hope Store…is the Nope Store. Natural Hopers Unite!"

Andrew asks the various speakers to take our places on stage. I'm glad that Kazu is beside me. I always feel safer when he's around. From time to time, friends wave to us from the auditorium and that relaxes me a bit. I imagine the rivers of dopamine coursing through the brains of all the "enhanced hopers" in the audience.

Andrew nods to us and moves to the podium. A tiny netbook rests on the podium. As the doors to the theatre close, the CNN logo appears on the huge TV monitor behind us. Then the title fades in with evocative music: "CNN PRESENTS: A TOWN HALL MEETING ON HOPE." People applaud jubilantly. Above the stage is a large garland trimmed with holiday lights and ornaments. Tis the season.

"Good evening, everyone. My name is Andrew Konstant. As the holidays are upon us, CNN wanted to bring you something a little different: 'A Town Hall Meeting on Hope.' We're coming to you live tonight from the hallowed halls of University of Chicago Medical Center, which has received several Nobel Prizes for their scientific discoveries. Thank you all for joining us."

Kazu and I give our opening remarks about the purpose of The Hope Store and the improved hope levels of our customers during our first three months since our doors opened. But Blair's remarks are less predictable, more combative. This is a town hall, but he's acting like it's a debate. Oh well.

"And now we'd like to open up the floor to the true stars of this town hall meeting: you, the audience," Andrew announces. "Let's bring up the house lights if we could." The house lights rise on the auditorium. "And what a good-looking audience you are," he says getting an easy laugh from the spectators. "We ask you to keep your questions brief and focused. Please give at least your name and also your affiliation if you wish. And don't be nervous. It's just the world watching." He smiles a winning smile. "Our first question comes from Ivan Fiddler who is a pastry chef. Welcome, sir, and please step up to the microphone."

A pleasant looking man in his thirties with buzzed black hair leans into the mic. At the same moment, his face also appears on the monitors. "Hello, I don't represent any big, fancy organization. I'm just a regular guy." Andrew says, "We like regular guys. Welcome, Ivan."

"Yes, well, in general, I like the idea of a Hope Store. I do. And I probably need to go there really soon myself." He laughs and the audience joins in too. "My question is this. How do you know hope installations really work? What if it's a placebo effect?"

"I'd like to take a stab at that if I may," I say. "There are three ways we measure improvement in our clients. Through anecdotal proof, behavioral proof, and scientific proof. Anecdotal proof is what clients tell us about what they experience, like if they feel more hopeful or empowered. Behavioral proof tracks new behaviors that clients achieve after treatment. And scientific proof is shown through a functional MRI which can actually track increases in dopamine levels in the brain which empower us to hope for things."

"I see you've avoided the hardest part of his question, about the placebo effect," says Blair Matters. "Isn't it true that in your clinical trials those who got true hope installations and those who got placebos *both* experienced relief from hopelessness?"

Kazu leans forward into the mic. "First, I'd like to acknowledge that Blair has recently done some excellent investigative reporting on The Hope Store. Here's the funny thing about placebos. The fact that people experience relief from a placebo is *not* proof that hope installations *don't* work. It simply proves that placebos *do* work. To avoid the placebo effect, we do MRI scanning of our clinical trial volunteers to quantify the dopamine levels. Only those with true hope installations show neurological enhancement."

"Wow, fascinating stuff," the moderator exclaims. "That deserves a town hall meeting of its own --"

Just then, the auditorium door opens and a handful of protestors carrying signs enter. The signs say, "NATURAL HOPERS UNITED." They are chanting different slogans: "The Hope Store is the The Hype Store." And "The mind is a terrible thing to medicate." "Nothing in life is free. The side effects are coming." Security guards converge on the group and usher them out. One agitator throws his posterboard sign high into the air above the audience. One man in the audience manages to catch the sign with one hand.

Andrew Konstant just shakes his head. "Well, all right then. We appreciate everyone's passion but this is live TV. Let's keep things moving. The next question comes from Tom Moseby who is a high school student at Our Lady Gate of Heaven."

A young man steps forward. He seems very poised for his age and the situation. "Hi, I'm Tom. As you can probably tell from my accent, I hail from the south. I wanted to come here today because I'm a Christian and I've heard a lot of religious leaders condemning The Hope Store." He laughs nervously. "I'm not used to public speaking."

"You're among friends," says Andrew. "And you're bringing a perspective to this national conversation we haven't heard yet. We have yet to hear from someone from the spiritual community."

"Well, I think if God were here today at this meeting...He'd give The Hope Store His blessings. I figure God's pretty busy so he'd appreciate the help." There is some cross-talk in the audience. "I disagree with those who've attacked The Hope Store and say the store is trying to replace God. I think they're both trying to accomplish the same thing."

An older man's voice shouts out from the balcony. "Since when do you speak on behalf of God? Where do you get off--"

A young woman shouts from the main floor seats, "Oh give me a friggin' break. Have you ever been hopeless yourself, dude?"

"The future's coming, people. Get out of the damned way!" the young woman shouts back.

Andrew intervenes. "I'd appreciate it if people did not speak out of turn or we're going to be here all night. Or security will have to remove you. So you were saying, Tom, that there is not a conflict between your religious views and The Hope Store?"

"No, sir. I don't think you can have too much of a good thing, do you?"

"Thank you for sharing," says the moderator. "Next we have Mimi Raines, a dissatisfied customer of the store."

The woman shyly approaches the microphone. She taps on the mic to make sure it's working. There is a thud. "Hi, I am a former customer of The Hope Store. I was terribly disappointed with my results. I did feel some bursts of hope and that was encouraging. But the goals that I hoped about did not come true. When I demanded my money back, The Hope Store refused to give me a refund."

Kazu is first to speak. "I'd like to respond to that. First, I'm sorry that you did not have a good experience at The Hope Store. I remember your case very well, Mimi. I think it's important to clarify that having hope does not guarantee you will achieve your goals. That's still up to you. Hope is the excitement of believing that you *can* achieve your goals. But the rest is up to you."

"I still want my money back," she says.

Andrew looks at his list. "The next question comes from Madrid Martinez. This should be interesting. Mr. Martinez is a very satisfied customer of The Hope Store. Welcome, sir."

The tall, dark and handsome Latino man approaches the microphone. He wears a black vest adorned with golden cherubs. "Thank you for taking my question tonight. In Spanish, The Hope Store translates as *tienda de esperanza* or *the store of hope*. For me, the store has lived up to its name. I am what is known in the hope industry as a 'good responder.' That means my hope levels have been through the roof, and I've had very few side effects." Madrid's eyes water for a moment and he appears to wipe away a tear.

"I wish you all knew me...a year ago. Hell, I wish you knew me a week ago. I'm changing every day! Having this new hope inside me, it goes beyond what you measure on a bar chart, it even goes beyond the job promotion I got at work last month. I used to wake up on a Monday morning absolutely dreading my factory job, but now a small voice inside me says, 'You can do this, Madrid. You've got this.' And I love how my friends who don't know about my hope installation say, 'Madrid, what's different about you? Did you lose weight? Did you get your hair cut? Are you in love?' Yeah, I'm in love all right. I'm in love with my life. I owe a lot of that to The Hope Store. If you've never been hopeless, I don't expect you to really understand how big this is. But other hope-challenged folks, you know what I'm talking about, 'cause we're part of the same tribe. So I guess my question is: why does the store have so many haters? I don't get that."

"I'd like to address that one if I may," says Blair. "First, I think the benefits you've gotten from this store indeed sound amazing. And I hope every customer who gets a hope installation gets terrific results as well. I really do." Blair smiles at Kazu and I. "I think some folks are just concerned that we should move a little slower, a little more cautiously when it comes to tricking the human brain. If I'm not mistaken, the next person on our audience list will deal head-on with this subject."

Andrew looks at his netbook. "Our next question comes from Robert Chang, who is with Natural Hopers United."

"Yes, this question is for Kazu Mori," starts Chang. "Isn't it true that during the clinical trials two of your subjects killed themselves after their hope installations? And if this is correct, how can you in good conscience provide a treatment to the public that can result in death?"

Kazu's face fills the TV monitors throughout the auditorium. I find myself, along with the rest of the TV audience, searching Kazu Mori's face for the answer.

LUKE

38. LOOSE CANNONS

Andrew Konstant jumps in because it is live TV after all. "Kazu, how do you respond to that question?"

"Out of respect for the privacy of the volunteers in our research study, I don't think it's appropriate to comment," says Kazu. I can see Chartreuse waiting in the wings. She is pacing back and forth.

Chang continues, "Let me be clear, I'm not asking whether suicidal thoughts and actions are a possible side effect of the hope treatment. That's clearly listed as one of the side effects on the release form that customers sign before treatment --"

"*Possible* side effects," Kazu says.

"Excuse me?" says Chang.

"It's a list of *possible* side effects," Kazu says. "It's very rare that customers will actually experience them. Less than 3%." He takes a sip of water. "And if I thought the treatment was dangerous, I promise you my partner and I would not have gotten hope installations ourselves. Which we have."

"I would also like the chance to ask a question of the Natural Hopers if I may," I say. You present your group, Mr. Chang, as a consumer advocate group concerned about the dangers of hope installation. And you want to raise awareness of natural ways to increase hope, is that right?"

"Yes, basically."

"You propose three things to access hope naturally: herbal remedies, physical exercise to stimulate endorphins, and cognitive therapy," I say. "But isn't it also true that you are funded by Nature's Way Herbals and Work Out World health clubs, and that you sit on the board of the Cognitive Behavior Therapists of Illinois?"

There is a stirring in the auditorium. Whispers. My point is well-received.

"Well, I don't recall it being a crime to volunteer to sit on a board, or to have donors to a cause," Chang says.

"Not a crime, but a conflict of interests," Kazu says. I can see people nodding.

"None of that changes my belief that there are safer, more natural ways to increase hope in people. Your list of possible side effects still includes mania, sleepwalking, liver failure, stroke, thoughts of suicide, and even death." Then Chang looks straight into the camera. "That's quite a list of nasty side effects. I don't think I'd want *my* wife to get a hope installation." He laughs.

"You might if your wife was hope-starved!" says a strong female voice from the main floor. I look over to see who is at the microphone stand.

It's Jada.

"And anyways, that would be *her* decision, not *yours*, wouldn't it, Mr. Chang?" Jada pauses dramatically for a moment. "Andrew, I'd like to speak if I could. I believe I am next on the list. My name is Jada Upshaw."

Andrew does a double-take at his guest list. He looks from one page to the next. Finally he says, "Yes, that's right. Jada Upshaw is next." Now I know for a fact that Jada is not on that list because I have that list in front of me. But I had talked about her at length to Andrew. I'm glad he's decided to play along. "Jada is a customer of The Hope Store who's had a very…unique response to treatment," he says.

Blair leans into the microphone. "I've interviewed Ms. Upshaw and know that she has also endured many debilitating side effects from her hope treatment."

"Thank you, Blair, but I'm quite capable of speaking for myself," she says.

"Jada, could you start by telling us why you turned to such an experimental procedure in the first place," says Andrew.

"Well, let me give the audience some background first. I've lived with hopelessness my whole life. I've not been helped by medication, exercise, therapy, or homeopathic remedies, thank you very much." She shoots a look at the Natural Hoper. "I've remained hopeless in spite of the love of my boyfriend and my family. I was born with a condition called *desina sperara.* It means I was born without the breath of hope."

Kazu and I turn to look at each other.

"When I first came to the store, I lied on the screening questionnaire. I said I didn't have that condition. The form clearly warned me that some clinical trial volunteers with desina sperara had very traumatic reactions to their hope installations. But I didn't want to be disqualified as a customer."

Kazu whispers into my ear.

"But to be perfectly frank, when I came to the store – I wasn't looking for hope. I was looking for revenge." I glance at Kazu's face and he looks worried.

"I'm confused," says Andrew. "Why revenge?"

"I was angry at all the people who dangled miracle cures in front of me, took my money, and dashed my hopes. And for full disclosure, I should share that I approached Blair Matters here to write an exposé on The Hope Store." The audience gasps collectively. Blair is turning pink. "But a funny thing happened on the way to The Hope Store. I found hope. Like Madrid here, I've had some amazing results, but I've had side effects too."

I turn to the moderator. "Andrew, Jada's story is rich and complicated. Would it be all right if she came up onstage?"

"Well...I don't want to put her on the spot," he says.

"I thought you'd never ask," Jada says, navigating her way through the auditorium. An usher helps her up the stairs to the stage. She takes a seat. "If I knew I was going to be on TV, I would've had my hair done at Van Cleefs." Some women in the audience chuckle.

"You look beautiful, Jada. Welcome," says Andrew, ever the charmer.

Blair is about to swallow his microphone. "Why don't we cut to the chase, Jada? You had some great results, but you had terrible side effects too -- sleepwalking and hallucinations, probably mania. And then you had a "hope extraction" on top of it. Care to comment?"

"I don't know if you, or anyone who has not lived a hopeless life, can understand this. Well, how could you?" Jada says. This self-assured Jada is not the stuttering woman I first encountered in my office on that October morning. "Thanks to The Hope Store, for the first time I've been able to get a glimpse of what a hope-driven life would look like. And now that I've seen that, I can't un-see it. Do you know what I mean?" She pauses. She looks into the audience. They seem to be on her side. "Wow, there are a lot of people here tonight."

"And how did you manage to deal with the side effects?" says Blair.

"My boyfriend Otis stays with me now and then, and most nights I just don't sleep at all. One night he took a hammer and nailed the sliding glass doors shut so I don't sleepwalk off my balcony." The audience laughs. "So I manage. I make do. And when all else fails in the wee hours of the night, I have something I've never had before. I have the memory of what a hope-driven life can be. And I owe that to The Hope Store." She locks eyes with Luke and Kazu.

"So what is it, Jada, that you found most problematic in your treatment? I know it's not been a walk in the park," Blair says.

"There *is* one drawback to the hope installation. And it's a big one."

The ears of the audience are trained on Jada. I fidget nervously with my papers because I have no idea where Jada is going with this. *Please, Jada, whatever you say...don't bring up your suicide attempts. Don't bring up your doppelgangers.*

Kazu looks at me. His Japanese eyebrows arch with concern. "Do you know what she's going to say?" he whispers.

"Not a clue," I whisper back. Under the table, I rub Kazu's knee.

The CNN cameras zoom in closer on Jada's expressive face.

"Here's what they don't tell you...maybe because they can't. But once you have that new hope inside you... you realize you have no excuses anymore. And that's scary because there's no one to blame. There's just you...and your own blinding potential. Along with your fears. A hope installation doesn't make you Superwoman. You still have to make things happen. You still have to do the work to make your dreams come true."

Both of us breathe a sigh of relief.

"Jada, I'm so glad you chose to share your story with us," says Andrew Konstant.

"Oh, one more thing," she says. I can hear emotion building in Jada's voice and I'm worried she's headed for a meltdown. "You people who want to shut down The Hope Store, the Natural Hopers and the skeptics...I don't know what world you live in, but the world I live in is not black and white. It's a million shades of gray. This store was never invented for you. It was invented for people like me. So with all due respect, you really should mind your own business, and leave The Hope Store for those who can benefit from it. The store may never save your life, but it may save the life of someone you love. That's all I wanted to say today." She hands the mic back to an usher. There is a spontaneous eruption of applause in the audience.

"Jada, I think love is an excellent place to end our town hall meeting on hope," gushes Andrew. Now he looks straight into the camera. His face appears on all screens. "We've just scratched the surface on the subject tonight. New breakthroughs in science happen every day. What would *you* do if you were hope-challenged? Would you live a life of quiet desperation? Would you take a yoga class? Or would you take a leap of faith into uncharted territory? I'm Andrew Konstant for CNN. This has been A Town Hall Meeting on Hope. Good night and happy holidays." The audience claps as the stage lights fade to black.

"That was terrific, really great," says Andrew. He looks at Jada and gives her a thumbs-up. The video screens cut to a commercial.

Jada stands up and rubs her forehead for a moment. She looks shaky like she might faint.

I run up to steady her, just in time.

JADA

39. A PARALLEL GIRL

After the town hall meeting, we all go out for a late dinner at Maggiano's. I apologize to everyone for almost fainting. I thank the universe I didn't collapse on live TV, tell folks I was light-headed because I hadn't eaten much during the day. But the truth is I don't know why I fainted. Could it be a side effect? What exactly is happening to me?

Everyone is congratulating me on my spontaneous remarks. Around the dinner table, people debate whether the viewers of the town hall will be more inclined to have a positive or negative view of The Hope Store. Did the Natural Hopers and Blair Matters cast sufficient doubt on the safety of hope installations? It's hard to say. The public is very fickle about things like this.

All I know is tonight I feel special. The last time I felt this special was when I took first place at the science fair for my diorama on the Great Chicago Fire. After dinner, I stay with Otis. I'm exhausted so Otis and I climb into bed. Still, we talk in the dark for about an hour because we're still wound up from the town hall.

In the middle of the night, I awaken and look at the clock: it's 3 a.m. When I roll over, I see Jada2 staring back at me with a big grin on her face. Where's Otis?

"Did you miss me?" she asks.

"I did actually. I didn't know if I'd see you again," I say. "Especially after the hope extraction."

"I caught your speech at the town hall meeting. Tres eloquent, girlfriend."

"Oh, I don't know," I say. "I just wanted to speak up on behalf of the Enhanced Hopers. And give the Natural Hopers a run for their money."

"You know, I came back to ask you a favor," she says. "I was thinking about you. I saw something in your future that worried me." A snow globe appears in her hand. "See that girl inside the globe? That's you." It does look a lot like me. This African American woman in blue green pajamas. "She's at a crossroads. She can give up…or she can carry on."

"I've been at that crossroads many times before," I say.

"So here's the favor -- don't give up. Carry on, will ya," says Jada2. "Do not pass go. Do not collect $200. Just keep on going."

"I'm not sure if I can make that promise, Jada2. I'm on shaky ground these days."

"I see. Shall I throw a pity party for you?"

"What?"

"Let me tell you a secret," she says. "You like secrets, don't you? See, half the battle of hoping is just refusing to give up…till you get what you want. It's not talent or luck or good genes so much as tenacity. That's the secret."

"Really?" I say.

"I hope to see you on the other side. Keep hope alive, Jada, by hook or by crook. If the technology is lagging, don't let your hope be dragging!"

I don't want Jada2 to leave yet. I have more questions for her. But I can't make her stay.

"Oh, and grow some balls. I did," she says with a smile. Then she unsnaps her pajama bottoms and lets them fall to the floor.

Jada2 has a penis.

And before I can say another word, she's gone. But Otis has returned.

"Otis," I say. He's deep asleep but I try to summon him. "I'm sorry for waking you…."

At first, he just mumbles something unintelligible. Finally, he opens one eye. "Are you having a nightmare?"

I throw my arms around him. I am not a hugger. I don't really like people touching me or touching other people. "Anything wrong?" he asks.

I say nothing. I just keep holding onto him so I don't fly away. So I don't turn into confetti or grow a penis like The Girl From My Parallel World.

"I don't know what's going to happen to me. I wrote a note, just to have it for a rainy day." I reach into my bag and pull out the paper. I hand it to Otis.

He takes the letter and begins reading.

Dear Otis,

   It's time. I always told you we were on borrowed time, didn't I?

   Thank you for loving me in spite of my shortcomings. And thank you for letting me love you in my own imperfect way. I know you don't believe in heaven or an afterlife, so I'll just say good-bye forever, Dear Heart. Have a great life.

   One way or another, I have to leave and there's nothing you can do about it. I've loved borrowing time with you.

Love,
Jada

LUKE

40. LUCKY PEOPLE

Kazu told me about a study he oversaw when he was working at LiveWell Laboratories. The study dealt with the nature of luck. Some years later, he would begin clinicals on hope installations and, of course, later meet me. In the luck study, researchers invited people who thought of themselves as lucky to be part of one test group, and people who thought of themselves as unlucky to be part of another test group. One at a time, subjects were placed alone in a room and told that they had lost their car keys and were running late for a romantic date with someone they were extremely excited to meet. They were told that it was crucial that they go by car and that taking a cab was not an option. They were told that they had no more than five minutes to find their keys or they would be late and their date would depart from their appointed meeting place. Then they were asked to find their keys as quickly as possible. Once they found the keys, the experiment was over.

The lucky people never stopped looking for their keys. They looked in a stunning array of places, including illogical places like in the refrigerator, in the pockets of clothing they weren't wearing, in rooms they hadn't been in, etc. More often than not these "lucky people" found the keys, often before the five minutes had elapsed.

The unlucky people, on the other hand, looked half-heartedly, looked in fairly obvious places like in the pockets of the clothes they were wearing, on the floor just around them, on nearby flat surfaces of tables. More often than not these "unlucky people" gave up before their five minutes were over and admitted defeat, letting the clock run out. Few of the unlucky subjects found their keys.

Both scenarios demonstrated the power of self-fulfilling prophecy, how we live up to our own expectations. But why do people consider themselves inherently lucky or unlucky? More importantly, Kazu wondered how the unlucky subjects could learn to become luckier, more hope-filled. How does the brain tell its owner -- biologically, chemically, electronically -- that it is lucky? Is there a way to trick the brain into thinking it is luckier, more hopeful, than it really is – thus increasing the owner's hope supply? And if so, what harm would there be in that?

For starters, Kazu showed both groups video footage of how each group searched for their keys which everyone found endlessly amusing. Much laughter ensued. Then the lucky and unlucky were able to ask each other questions.

One lucky person asked an unlucky person why they only searched the floor in the immediate area. The unlucky person said they assumed that the keys would have fallen nearby. One unlucky person asked a lucky person why they looked in illogical places like the refrigerator and rooms they hadn't been in. The lucky person said that often she loses things when she is not paying attention. Besides, she really wanted to make it to that hot date on time. Invariably, the lucky person kept the reward of the hot date upmost in his mind and took it seriously.

Kazu then asked both groups how they came to think of themselves as lucky or not. He asked the unlucky ones what it would take to start thinking of themselves as lucky people. By the end of the six-week study, many of the unluckies became better at finding the cars keys and finding opportunities in general. More importantly, many unluckies started to think of themselves as lucky for the first time in their lives.

LUKE

41. A PRIVATE PERSON

Jada Upshaw did us proud at the town hall. Twitter crowned her the new Queen of Hope. Websites started popping up devoted to all things Jada. But Jada wasn't having any of it. Instead of hearing how the audience had rooted and clapped for her, she felt she'd made a fool of herself, that she had gone from national cover girl for hope to a terrible responder with horrible side effects and zero hope.

"I'm just tired all the time," she says.

I encourage her to watch the broadcast of the town hall meeting with me. "Luke, you have to understand, I'm a private person and I've been forced to strip naked in public. My most personal secrets are joked about on late-night talk shows. I can't go anywhere without being asked for my, uh, uh, what do you call it when you, uh, sign something. Autograph! They ask me for my damn autograph." Jada is stuttering again, forgetting simple words. She hasn't done that since her hope installation.

The day after the town hall, our email box is flooded with requests for appointments. And, sure, there is some hate mail too. Haters are always gonna hate. It's their calling. But from the looks of it, things are looking up for this little store of ours. If The Hope Store wasn't on the map before, it certainly is now after CNN's Town Hall Meeting on Hope. In spite of serious concerns about Jada and a few others with side effects, we are growing. A reporter for Crains' Business called just today. He wanted to know if we are considering franchising The Hope Store.

I'm feeling overwhelmed so I dial the one number that can save me. "Kazu?" I say into my phone. "I just wanted to hear your voice."

"Where are you, Luke? You don't sound so great."

"I just wanted to hear your voice. We're okay, aren't we?" I say.

"What do you mean?" says Kazu.

"Things have been busy with the town hall and stuff. We haven't had a lot of *us time*. So I just want to make sure we're okay."

"I think we've both been pretty stressed," he says. "But if two people with hope installations can't keep their acts together, who can?" He laughs his mad scientist laugh. I chuckle.

"Who can indeed," I say. "I'll be home soon."
We hang up. My phone rings again.

"Kazu?" I say.

"Are you sitting down?" It's not Kazu. It's
Chartreuse.

"What is it, Chartreuse? What can I do for
you?" If she has one more critical comment to make,
I will just slowly hang up the phone.

"I talked to our accountant today. We're in the
black. We're turning a profit and quite a good one.
Seems the town hall meeting really put us on the
map. We were the topic of every water cooler
discussion, every blog and newspaper editorial. Side
effects and all. I guess you're right that any press is
good press."

"We're turning a profit? That's fantastic,
Chartreuse," I say. "Does that mean we're getting
funding for the new year?"

"We're getting close to making a decision. I'll
keep you posted."

⋰★⋱

For one full week, Jada Upshaw has been a
missing person. It's as if her wish had come true: to
be one of the Disappeared, one of the lost girls. Otis
files a missing persons report with the police. Kazu
and I cuddle on the sofa as we watch "Nightline."
My cell rings. I'm tempted to let it go to voicemail,
but I don't.

It's Blair Matters.

"Luke, you haven't found Jada yet, have you?"

"No. Have you heard from her?"

"Not exactly. But I think I know where she is."

LUKE

42. CLOSE YOUR EYES

"What do you mean you think you know where she is?!" I say. I'm losing my patience, to say nothing of my sanity.

"I can't get into that right now," says Blair. "But check the roof of The Hope Store building."

"The roof? Why the –"

"She may be suicidal. I'm afraid she might jump off the roof of The Hope Store!" he says. "Talk about a publicity nightmare," and he hangs up.

I climb into the car and drive to the store. I turn on the store lights and take the stairs up three flights to the roof, push open the heavy iron door which opens to the rooftop. At first, I see nothing. I see the roof, some stars, a couple of white plastic chairs. I'm just about to leave when I hear someone clear her throat.

And there standing at the edge of the roof, blending into the sky in her navy blue dress, is Jada. She just stands there hypnotized, looking out over the city.

"Jada!" I shout. I approach her. "I've been looking all over for you. What're you doing up here?"

She does not turn to look at me. "Have you ever noticed you can see the red Target sign from here?" Her voice is very calm as she speaks.

"No, I never noticed, Jada. But I think we should –"

"Don't get me wrong. I like Target, like that they have a Starbucks inside and a grocery store with fresh fruit, they got nice kitchenware and beddings upstairs. You go into Target for a teal hand towel and come out with a full week's groceries, three CD's by Adele, and if you're lucky – you might remember the hand towel."

"Jada, I'm so happy to see you!" I say. "Everyone's been worried about you. We've all been looking for you."

"I'm right here. Can't you see me? All you have to do is look." There is an edge to her tone that is unfamiliar.

"Jada, I'd like to talk about how you're doing. I think that's what's important –"

"I'm getting there, Lukester. Don't rush me. Have I ever told you how much I hate when you rush me?" she says staring me down.

"Yes, you've told me. I'm sorry --"

"And anyway, my idea of hope doesn't have to be your idea of hope, you know?"

I wonder if Blair has called the cops by now. "What are you saying, Jada?"

"I don't know. I guess I'm confused…by my hope treatment…by what's happening to me. I'd be lying if I said I wasn't deeply disappointed. And I don't want to lie anymore." She reaches into her bag and takes out a little origami paper bird. She kisses it gently, throws it off the roof.

"We should talk about this," I say. "It's important."

"Who knows? Maybe I'll be back at the store next month. Or maybe I'll just…call it a day. Maybe I'll finally have a successful suicide."

I'm trying to think of something helpful to say but no words come.

"These little origami cranes are part of my farewell ritual. The birds are here to carry my spirit from this world into the next one. Hopefully it will be a better world. Luke, you have to promise me if I ever do manage to take my life…that you won't feel in any way… responsible. Because you're not."

I look at the skyline.

"You know what I like about origami? You take this perfectly ordinary, perfectly flat sheet of paper. And you begin folding it until it becomes something totally unique. It's a transformation story," she says.

"I've always rooted for you, Jada. I still do. Hey, how about we get off this rooftop before one of us blows away." I start to move toward the door, but Jada stays put.

"You asked me what I'm doing up here. You told me once that the view was beautiful up here at night. I wanted to see for myself." A breeze blows and Jada's hat flies off the roof.

"Your hat."

She walks to the edge of the roof and watches her hat slowly descend three stories.

"For two amazing weeks, I knew what it was like to have hope. To look forward to the day! It was amazing. And then poof! Something happened. What happened, Luke?"

"I don't know, Jada. I wish I knew."

"It's worse now, Luke, to know what hope feels like, what I've been missing out on. Sometimes I hate you for what you did to me."

"It was always for you, Jada."

She surveys the Chicago skyline. "Do you think our brains can fix themselves?" she asks. "The human body fixes itself all the time. I don't see why the brain would be any different. When I started treatment in October, I promised to give myself three months. If the installation didn't work by end of December – I was going to kill myself. I couldn't bear to start another year."

"I don't want to lose you, Jada." I am trying to read her face.

"Yeah, I'm a good customer," she says.

"You're more than that," I say. She smiles.

Suddenly the rooftop door creaks open. It's Kazu. "There you two are! Am I glad to see you, Jada," he says. Kazu embraces her.

"What's going on?" she asks. Now Otis steps through the door, followed by Blair Matters. It's a small parade.

"Jada, sweetheart," Otis starts. "They're holding a table for us at the Grand Lux...whenever you're ready to have dinner with me again."

She shakes her head defiantly. "This better not be an intervention or I'm going to be very pissed."

Jada walks over to me. She speaks just loud enough for me to hear. "Tell me something. How many people, Luke?" she says. "How many people are on this damn roof?"

"What do you mean?"

"I've been hallucinating a bit lately. So is it just the two of us here, or are there others?"

I look around and count them one by one. "I count five."

"Well, that's three too many!!"

Blair jumps in. "Jada, it was inspiring talking with you at the town hall meeting. A producer friend of mine at Bravo was watching too and would love to do a reality show that follows your trials and tribulations at The Hope Store. You'd be paid handsomely." Blair produces a sheet of paper and pen and offers it to her. "All you have to do is sign this agreement which states you give Bravo permission to create the show. And that you're gravely   concerned that The Hope Store put your health in jeopardy."

She looks directly into Blair's eyes. "I never said the store put me in jeopardy. I knew the procedure had risks. That was never a question."

"Of course, you don't have to sign, Jada," Blair continues. "You can walk away from this chance to tell your story. You can even walk away from the money if you dare."

Out of the corner of my eye, I'm aware that Otis and Kazu are listening with great interest.

"It's tempting. I guess I could buy the condo they're trying to evict me from," she says looking at Otis. I can almost hear the wheels of her brain turning. "I could stop worrying about money and start enjoying life," she says. I'm heartsick at the thought that Jada is actually falling for Blair Matters' offer.

"Let's say you pass on the offer. What would the rest of your life look like?" says Blair. "You wake up tomorrow with your side effects and you ride The Hope Store roller-coaster. And maybe because you didn't do the Bravo show, maybe hundreds of customers come to the store and wind up with horrible, life-threatening side effects. It's not your fault. No one would ever blame you. But with this show, you could be a consumer advocate. You could make sure that the choices the public makes are educated choices."

Jada nods slowly. "This is a very big decision. I'm going to have to ask you to let me sleep on it tonight."

"No can do. The Bravo exec wants a decision tonight, or the deal is off."

She ponders a bit, looks at Otis, Luke and Kazu. "Then the answer is no. Final answer."

Blair seems flustered, looks like he wants to spit at something. "Opportunities don't come along like this very often. But whatever. It's your loss."

Then a big smile spreads across Jada's face. "No, the loss is completely yours, Blair."

He shakes his head in disgust and makes his way toward the stairwell.

"Otis, Kazu, could you wait for us downstairs?" I say. "I'd like a moment to talk with Jada if that's okay."

"It's almost midnight!" Kazu says.

"We'll be down soon."

The men nod and make their way toward the stairwell. And then it's just us again.

She fishes a piece of paper from her purse and scribbles a note on it. Then, with lightning speed, she folds the sheet into a shape. I watch her as always with great interest. Not as a kid watches a bug in a jar, but as a friend watches a friend. And we are friends. Why deny it?

Whistles and laughter bubble up from the revelers on the street below.

Jada walks up to me, looks deep into my eyes for a moment. "Luke, do you trust me?" The wind picks up a bit.

"Of course I do." She smiles back.

"Close your eyes," she says.

"Why?"

"Because I asked you to?"

Down below on Clark Street, I hear the crowd start to shout out the final countdown: "10...9..."

"I'm not comfortable closing my eyes right now."

"Damn it, Luke, I know you hate not having control. But I have to win sometimes. It's something friends do for each other."

"8...7..."

And now I'm getting nervous. I worry that Jada might jump off the roof, might take her life. But she sounds so reasonable, so reassuring.

"I want to thank you and Kazu for trying to help me," she says.

"6... 5..."

She seems to be getting emotional. She flashes a radiant smile, more radiant than I've ever seen her smile. She looks...happy.

"Now be a good boy and close your eyes. Trust me, everything is going to be fine."

"4... 3..."

With reservations, I close my eyes but I peek a little. Jada gently places something in my hand. I'm relieved to see her walking toward the stairwell and not the edge of the roof.

"2...1...HAPPY NEW YEAR!!!" The crowd below goes wild, fireworks illuminate the city, revelers blow their toy horns. I open my eyes and Jada's gone. Here I stand alone on the rooftop with a folded piece of paper. It's an origami crane. I unfold it, flap by flap. In Jada's familiar scrawl is a note:

NO TO BRAVO.
YES TO THE HOPE STORE.
SEE YOU FRIDAY AT 2 PM.
TRY AGAIN?

I breathe a deep sigh of relief. I'm thrilled Jada has chosen to live, has chosen to work with us again even after our failings. This optimism doesn't come from magnetic fields or slow-falling confetti.

It comes from her.

JADA

43. STILL HERE

I make my way down the three flights of stairs. I try to picture Luke unfolding my paper bird and it makes me smile.

Sometimes things happen you can't explain... because they happen only to you and no one else. And who else would really understand? Maybe you believe in a store, or a person, or an idea. Maybe you just believe in a singer you heard once on the radio because she was amazing...and you believe she can be amazing again. That's how I feel about myself tonight: that I can be amazing again.

For two weeks I knew what it was like to have hope, to have a waterfall of dopamine flowing inside me, cascading into whole new places. Once you see your own shining possibilities, you can't un-see them. And why would you want to?

I live in a brave new world these days divided into the Natural Hopers (those who only believe in the hope you're born with) and the Enhanced Hopers (those who believe in everything else). People gather around watercoolers all over the world and debate whether hope installations are a good thing or a bad thing. I, for one, think they are a good thing.

It's a new year and contrary to all my predictions -- I'm still here, still trying to find my rightful place in the world. I've learned that as long as I have even just a little bit of hope...

When I get to ground level, Otis is waiting patiently on the sidewalk for me.

We go to his place and order in, watch the fireworks on TV and cuddle on the sofa. We toast our glasses of sparkling grape juice to the future.

Out of the corner of my eye, I see a body dangling from a rope from the ceiling. It's Jada2. Her body slowly turns as if blown by a breeze. Her eyes blink open and she smiles at me. She blows me a kiss. With each revolution, her image becomes fainter and fainter until she is gone.

I will find a way to be happy this year if it's the last thing I do.

I used to think of myself as a falling star, a constellation of possibilities that would never amount to anything. And falling stars were sad because they were falling after all. But recently I googled the term. It said falling stars are also called *shooting stars*. How weird is that? I guess it's all in how you look at things... that make them what they are.

LUKE

44. CHOPPER

I'm getting cold up here on this roof all by myself. My smartphone sings to me its little song. It's Kazu. He's still waiting downstairs and would love to go out for Japanese food. I can't wait to tell him about Jada, that she hasn't given up hope. This store is going to help a lot of people. *We're* going to help a lot of people.

And while I'm at it, I should mention to Kazu how much I love him and how super cute he is and how I divide my life into two parts -- Before Kazu and After Kazu -- and how the after part is so much better and it's not like how in the movies where one lover tells the other: "You complete me" because what Kazu did, what he truly did, was give me the tools to complete myself, you see, so assembly was required on my part.

I should tell him that.

I *will* tell him that.

Right after I give him a big, juicy New Year's kiss.

And now I imagine a chopper hovering over the rooftop and lifting up and away. The Bravo cameraman on-board surely will get some footage of a man on a rooftop walking toward a door. That man would be me. Credits would roll right about now if this was a series on Bravo -- and who's to say it shouldn't be? Clocks everywhere in Chicago have struck twelve and the reveling goes and this is what some of the people here tonight may have overlooked in the night's commotion: the sky filling with light, fireworks transforming night into day...the birth of a new year.

ACKNOWLEDGEMENTS

Thank you to my readers. Without you, I am shouting into the void.

Gratitude to my writing group Ouija Board (David C. Taylor, Alison DeLuca, Randy Tatano, Stephanie Baird and others) and for my beta readers: Alison DeLuca and the late JT Kalnay. For support from Michael Jones, Nancy Andria, Mary Corcoran, Jade Ham, Lorraine Harrell, Susan Namest, and many others. To Rosie Cook whose quirky personality was inspiration for Jada Upshaw. To Kazu Inoue for his friendship over the years. To my Buddhist practice for providing me the wisdom to know what to do, and the courage to act on the wisdom.

As always thanks to my manager Nicholas Bogner of Affirmative Entertainment who seeks to bring my books to the big screen. My first novel *The Prospect of My Arrival* was a finalist in the Amazon Breakthrough Novel Awards. Thanks to the Kindle Storyteller Contest for motivating me to send my book out into the world sooner than I would have.

The cover design was based on an image created by Acetyl "Rachel" Choline. I'm grateful to designer Bogdan Ghigeanu who worked with me to create the final image. The interior vintage brain image was by designer Cathy Hull. Special thanks to Randy Tatano for nagging me to get this novel into print. The poetry excerpts in the section headers are from my book *Crossing with the Light* (Tia Chucha Press).

On the subject of hope, I inherited my mother's optimism and my father's scientific curiosity and they have served me well through the dark nights. Every day we learn more about the wonders of the human brain, so I don't think my story is all that unlikely. With any luck, one day a Hope Store will be coming soon to a neighborhood near you.

ABOUT THE AUTHOR

Dwight Okita lives in Chicago with an imaginary cat and a great circle of friends. He also designs websites, is a professional therapeutic cuddler, a Nichiren Buddhist, and a passionate moviegoer. Dwight envisions a world more beautiful than this one and is confident we will manage to create it together in this lifetime.

Nicholas Bogner of Affirmative Entertainment, Dwight's manager in Hollywood, works to get his books onto the big screen. Currently, the author is writing a novel called EVERY TIME WE SAY GOODBYE which deals with love, reincarnation, and the gun violence epidemic.

He is especially grateful that you, Dear Reader, have chosen to read this book.

You might also enjoy his first novel *The Prospect of My Arrival* and his poetry book *Crossing with the Light*. You can reach the author at his website: **www.DwightOkita.com**

Made in the USA
Lexington, KY
16 January 2018